OUR CARRION HEARTS

BY BRIAN FATAH STEELE

READ UNTIL YOU BLEED!

BRIAN FATAH STEELE

OUR CARRION HEARTS

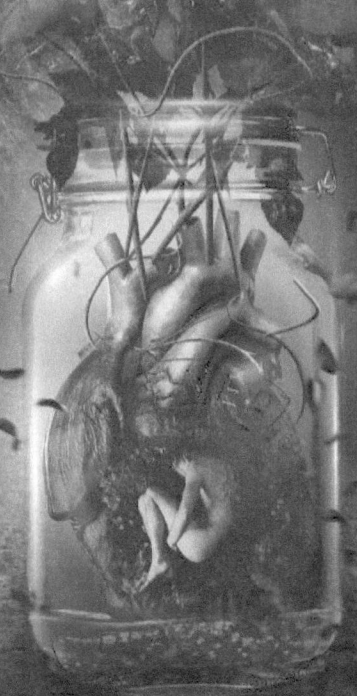

For Dan and Brittany.
Thank you both for everything.

ACKNOWLEDGEMENTS

This novel is lot different from my previous ones. I wanted to write something darker, more visceral. Hopefully readers understand what I was trying to do here.

A lot of people need thanked, and I'll likely forget some people. Jonathan Joyce was beta-reader and proofed the book, making it presentable. Dan and Brittany Weymouth were always there with coffee and support, which is why I brutally killed them off as characters in the book. Elizabeth Tussey helped me with the title after I struggled with it. Annie Joyce, Joe Shaffer, Kendell Gibson, and Sierra Jones – thank you. Detective John Headley of the East Liverpool Police Department was gracious enough to answer dozens of my procedural questions, and I can't thank him enough. Any mistakes concerning the law enforcement portions of the story are either my own or done purposely.

I'm not going to name drop all the people within our amazing horror community that made this book possible. You know who you are and I appreciate each and every one of you for your support. I can only hope I give it back well enough in kind.

This entire novel was written to the folk-metal music of Danheim.

A huge shout out to my Mom and Dad for continuing to put up with my nonsense. Nathan, Jordan, and Quintin, thanks for being awesome "little" brothers. Miss you Adam. Hopefully my sisters-in-laws will keep you in line, my nephews keeping you busy.

PROLOGUE

When humanity separated itself from the beasts, so did The Carrion Court separate itself from humanity. Older, stronger, we are the things that lurked in the darkness just beyond the light of the fire. The form of man had been taken at some point in distant history to better adapt us, but we were never one with mankind. We used their form to enable us to feed off the humans in different fashions; picking at their remains as we slowly built societies for ourselves on the land they thought they owned.

We find the name given to ourselves back in the late 14th century to be quite fitting and not a bit amusing, don't you think?

You see, that was when our Five Tribes came to an accord and found a lasting peace. Many would argue it was due to the leadership of the time, but others say it was due to the will of our gods. They desired unity and made it so on earth. Scoff if you might, I try not to get on the bad side of ravenous deities.

Yes, I know, you're fully aware of whom I speak, but allow me my monologue.

Manaha guides the Kin into The Mist and their transformation into the Wendigo, where they feed upon flesh. Pith teaches the Sect, often known as Witches, in their spell casting so that they might extract fear. Great Vbenne is the force behind the Sallow, most commonly known as Vampires, in their quest to consume blood. Larcre is lord to the Throng, the vast armada of Fey, who find satisfaction in belief. Finally, we have Crozen who watches over the Vacant, the powerful Djinn, and their hunger for souls.

We, the powerful and terrible, were given these gifts by insatiable entities who linger at the edges of our reality. On this planet, we are here to feed as each of our kind is wont to do. There is to be no politicking or squabbling, no betrayal or dramatics.

Such outbursts for attention are unnecessary. Also, I do not care.

Now, enlighten us: I wish to know how this idiocy came to fruition.

CHAPTER 1

DANIEL

I suppose I'll open at the point when I was eating a homeless man behind a Chinese restaurant in Florida. It's as good a place as any.

* * *

It was this little alleyway, smelled like fried rice and peanut oil. Not too terrible of a smell, all things considered. I was shortcutting through when I saw the guy. It was about 3am. He was asleep and curled up next to a dumpster. No one was out on the street, and the restaurant closed several hours earlier.

This wasn't a clean alley, and this wasn't a clean man. Filth littered every corner of the space, crawling into the crevices between the bricks. The asphalt had myriad grease stains running across it where it they weren't interrupted by cracks. Bags of detritus left unattended for months shifted in the presence of rats, a miasma of rotting food wavering off the top of the dumpster. Debris spilled out everywhere, trails of it in every direction. Some of it had splattered against the far wall, probably when the garbage truck hastily came to retrieve the dumpster. A single light above the top of the restaurant's back door was illuminated through the gloom. The human laying next to the big green dumpster had on crusted jeans, torn shoes, and a shirt of indistinguishable color. His hair and beard hadn't been trimmed in years, by my glance.

He was out, too. Snoring away. If I had been a better person, a different person, I would have left him to sleep. But I wasn't. I crept over and pulled the knife from where it was concealed in my pant leg. He never knew I was coming.

One quick jab to his exposed neck towards his jugular and a slow drag across. His eyes popped open and I turned him to the ground quickly. I didn't want any of that blood spraying out on me. He flailed for a minute, but I held him down. It didn't take long. Then I rolled him over and went to work, fast, before anyone else decided to take a shortcut through.

I slit open his abdomen and pulled out a few organs. I had my preferences on taste. I nibbled on a sliver of belly-flesh as I pocketed the kidneys and liver for later. The heart, I began eating right then as I casually kicked the rest of the corpse back behind the dumpster. Fresh heart is the best, it's clean tasting and the metallic sweetness of iron-rich blood is as satisfying to cravings as a bowl of candy. The kidney and liver should be rinsed anyway, but these had an especially musky whiff, their donor was an addict of some sort, probably. No one would notice the body for a few days, especially with the stench already so strong. That damn left-hand kept flopping back out, and I had to reach down to hide it better underneath the weight of the torso.

I was glancing into the dumpster to look for something like an old towel, or newspaper to wipe my hands off on when my phone rang. My phone never rang, and I couldn't even think of a person who would want to call me, let alone at this hour. I ignored it and let it go to voice mail, assuming it was a wrong number. I found some used napkins in the Chinese restaurant's bags, and got most of the blood off, wiping down the liver and kidneys. I don't know why I bothered at this; the organs already deposited crimson stains on my suit coat pocket now. Strolling out of the alleyway with my treats, I felt pretty good about how my night had ended. Then my phone rang again.

Now I was annoyed. I reached into my pocket to pull it out, ready to yell at someone. Needless to say, I was surprised to see Rosenthal's name on the caller ID. I tossed the last of the candy-like heart into my mouth and answered while still chewing.

"What?"

"Where are you?"

"Florida."

"Shit. When's the last time the Spirit called you?"

"I dunno, been a while. Almost a year. Why?"

"Don't go into The Mist. Come home, we have a situation. Stay out of The Mist in the meantime."

"Are you serious? I can't..."

"Daniel, this is worth the risk. Come home."

And he hung up.

I stared at the phone wondering what kind of cryptic shit I had just gotten myself into.

*   *   *

To be perfectly honest, if I needed a car, I would simply steal one. It's a lot easier than you think. Especially when you look like me. I walk up, smile, they slip the car keys into my hand, and even say "thank you." I usually don't keep the cars for long, just to get from point A to point B. It's nothing personal, but it's a "lifestyle choice" as they say.

But driving almost 17 hours from Miami, Florida to Opal, Indiana would take more than a stolen car. The risk of it wasn't an issue, I needed something that wouldn't be noticed. Too risky. That was fine, I had access to millions of dollars. I needed to find a shady car dealer. Someone who would take cash fast and ask no questions. Such a lot was found near Sweetwater, at "Benedict's Used". But I needed to get cleaned-up at my place before I went there, as it's frowned upon to go out in public with blood stains on your clothes.

Benedict was himself the physical embodiment of a caricature drawing – bulging gut, cowboy hat, with a persistent sunburn in the face. For an extra five thousand under the table, certain paperwork simply vanished. I was now the proud owner of a Toyota sedan, nothing too flashy, that would definitely get me back to Indiana.

The whole transaction would've been a lot easier twenty years ago. I'm usually never nostalgic except when it comes to crime. Too many advancements in forensics for my tastes these days. Investigative techniques today make theft and murder damn hard, turns policing into a lot less detective work and more of a science. At least I used to have some begrudging respect for the detectives picking through the clues I'd left. Now it's guys in lab coats, and they're stuck in an office, disconnected from the actual scene.

I had just eaten the kidneys before I dealt with getting a new car. It's bad to negotiate when you're hangry. A quick stop back at the loft I rented to pack and I could be on my way, since I had already showered off the blood before my trip to the car lot. A few changes of clothes, toiletries, phone charger, that stuff. I knew I should probably dress down for Indiana, so I only brought one suit along with the one I was wearing, and I packed a few jeans and t-shirts. I really didn't know what to expect. Since I had eaten a decent amount, I'd be able to power through the day and night in a single trip.

The car zoomed off up the highway and I hooked my phone up to the car stereo. My kind must always be able to adapt, stagnation leads to death. It was nothing for me to tap on the music app on my phone and pull up streaming radio. It was still sunny Florida September, so, I let Avicii, Bassnectar, and Nero fill the car.

And I just drove.

CHAPTER 2

KELSEY

I don't know... where do you want me to start? Does it really matter? Fuck you.

*   *   *

Sunlight drifted through the window, catching the dust drifting through the air. It all had a faint green hue thanks to the new curtains I stapled to the window frame a few months back. It was kind of pretty in a way. I wasn't sleeping much anymore thanks to my condition, but Jeff was happily snoring away next to me. He was always relatively happy it seemed.

I slipped out of the sheets and carefully got out of bed. Not wanting to wake him, I quietly made my way out of the bedroom towards the bathroom. I took a brush to my hair while I taking my morning piss. My hand found the small swell of my belly and the two-month-old baby growing there. I was a pretty skinny girl, so, I was showing already more visibly than some would. Finishing up, I glanced around for anything that would do for clothes. I've been out growing my wardrobe and haven't felt like buying anything new since I was just gonna outgrow that shit. A pair of gym shorts lay thrown over the tub, and I knew there was a tank top still sitting on the couch from a few days ago. Good enough.

The trailer was a wreck. It had been since the day Jeff and I moved in with each other. He never bothered to clean, and it always seemed that I was too busy, or lately, just too tired. Sometimes it bothered me, but usually I didn't care. I was more worried about when the baby came. When she came. We all knew it was going to be a girl. At the moment, the issue with the trailer's mess was that I couldn't find a hair tie. Dealing with Jeff this early in the morning really wasn't an option, so I didn't want to tear through the place looking for one and risk waking him.

Shrugging, I grabbed a rubber band out of the junk drawer and grimaced as I pulled up my shoulder length dyed black hair.

Heading outside to take in some fresh-air, I squinted in the sun. Jeff had called my parents' property a "compound" once, but it was hardly that. The big, two-story house the rest of the family lived in was slowly falling apart, our trailer, five overhangs that barely counted as garages, two sheds that never got used, and what was lovingly referred to as "the shack." It all took up about an acre and, with another four acres owned. The Radu family might be white trash, but they had land. Granted, Ennis, Ohio was in the rural and impoverished part of the state referred to as "Appalachia," but it was more than most people could lay claim to.

My dad was leaving the house to go to work, his tow truck was already idling. He wasn't a big man, but he was sturdy. Handsome, too. I had gotten my willowy figure and olive skin from him.

"How's my big girl?" he asked.

"Just waking up," I replied.

"Another day, another dream," he said with a laugh.

"What's the house like today?"

His smile faded. "Your mom is having one of her 'episodes'. Grandma Judy isn't helping. Think Tessa is still asleep."

Mom had an 'episode' seemingly every day anymore.

"Don't you worry none about it," he said, giving me a hug. "You take care of your business."

"Thanks, dad."

He walked off to his tow truck, and I headed to the shack.

I don't know why we called it that, as it was hardly a shack. It was a solidly built structure made of cinder block that twenty-by-twelve feet and twelve feet high with a wood roof. It even had singles. It had a dirt floor, but that was more for effect. I should mention we could shackle six people to the walls and a person each to the two support beams. Not that we ever had more than four people captured at once, but it paid to be prepared. There was electricity for lights, water for a small sink, and two large tables full of all types of fun toys.

None of that interested me at the moment, nor did the attractive blonde college student I had bound in the dirt. I'd get back to her. I passed all the distraction to the back of the shack, where a desiccated corpse hung lovingly preserved. A young woman not much older than me, dressed in a gown and adorn with oils and spices, magical symbols of our people painstakingly painted in ritual all over her now dried skin. It was my older sister, Ruby. She had died in a reckless attempt at spell casting, but now found a new purpose in death. I knelt down before the body of my dead sister we used as a shrine and began my morning prayer.

"Beloved Pith, whisper to me."

"I give myself over to you."

"Kelsey Anne Radu, your servant."

"Your will, your Sect."

"Let the fear flow upon us."

"In your name, in your honor."

I stood up, feeling stronger in my devotion. Unlike some other Tribes, I knew my god was real. Unlike some members of another Sect, I had actually spoken to Pith. Oh yes, there was a plan.

Now I could entertain myself.

The young woman's name was Summer, which I found delightful. Tan, blonde hair, light freckles, toned body. Of course, her name was Summer. I had already ripped out half of her hair and carved out a few of the freckles on her chest. The Fear that slicing those fleshy bits had caused made those pieces taste delicious. Usually, as a Sect, we would suck the Fear from our captives out of their mouths in those bluish-grey, ethereal plumes, as it appeared and swallow it down. Now, by myself, I was only keeping the bare minimum for myself, depositing the rest into the mouth of Ruby to sustain her spirit. The smaller feedings might have been a problem for me and the baby; but we've killed over twenty people in the last four months. Usually one full feeding is more than enough.

Summer sobbed as I crouched down in front of her. The vestige of her former beauty was still apparent even after what I had put her through. Good. All she had on was a pair of soiled underwear as she pushed back a few inches from me.

"I'm bored of your freckles, Summer. I think it's time we removed something bigger," I said as I eyed her left nipple.

"Maybe something you don't really need. I'm going to want to keep you around for a while longer."

She began to scream as I went up to retrieve a pair of shears.

CHAPTER 3

DANIEL

Eighteen hours later, I was pulling into Opal city limits. It was small town of only about eight thousand people, but it did alright. It looked a little bit more worn down since the last time I was here, though. Maybe that was just the early dawn light. I wove my way through familiar streets, passing the school I used to attend and the doctor's office I had gone to, leaving behind these passing memories I had from long ago. This wasn't my life anymore, and with good reason. These people couldn't know me, couldn't know Daniel Hale. It was too dangerous for everyone.

I still looked twenty-four even though I was in my forties now. I lived a life none of these people could hope to understand. Few could. It was one of blood and Mist. The experiences of my life which I called "home" now, laid outside the realm of reason and comfort.

Leaving the confines of the Opal town-limits, I headed out towards the forest to find my Kin. This was where the Rosenthal's estate sat. It was large, but not opulent, and took up twenty-two acres of woodland a few miles north of Opal. The house sat here for generations, always owned by a member of the Rosenthal clan. The house had three stories; it was a sprawling white colonial manor with several out-buildings. Rosenthal manor was long and narrow, it sat back a bit from the road, and the drive was lined by trees. Every time I arrived, the view of the place moved me. It appeared like a pale mirage out of the green foliage, as it wavering into sight, giving a slightly majestic appearance.

I pulled up in the gravel outside the main house and parked. Stretching as I stood up from the car seat, I stared around at the land. Florida was beautiful, but nothing beat the primal wilderness of my home. I had missed it. I always forgot how much I missed it until I returned. The sun peeked over; the sky was a clear blue. It was late spring, and the budding leaves were flourishing on all the trees.   There were birds singing everywhere. The natural air smelled so clean, like crisp pine sap and fresh dew.

I had lived in Miami for a few years and tried staying off the grid as best I could. Miami was garish and loud; it was a great place to party but I had never called it home. I had never called anywhere home but Opal. Not New York, not London, not that little town on the coast of Northern California. Miami had just been another place to stop along the way for a while, in my ongoing adventures. I had no connections to it or to the people there. Not like here, Opal was my home.

If Rosenthal kept to his old habits, he would be having his coffee and reading today's newspaper on the back porch around this time. Likely reading the news on a tablet now. I made my way around the sprawling house to the backyard, smiling when I saw him sipping on a mug.

Gerald Rosenthal appeared in fifties but he was much older than that. Tall and thin with short-cropped grey hair, he appeared to have a serious demeanor. But he was one of the most kind, if not aloof, people I'd ever met. He was my mentor as well as a friend.

"Daniel," he said, coming around the table. "I'm glad you could make it."

"Well, you made it seem pretty urgent."

"It is, sit. Would you like any coffee?"

"No, I'm going to have to crash here soon, I drove straight from Miami. Just tell me what's going on."

Rosenthal sighed. "It's a number of things, which are possibly all connected. The most disturbing thing is that The Elders have gone quiet."

"They weren't exactly forthcoming before."

"This is different. Their last few communications were erratic nonsense. All of them were talking in near gibberish."

That gave me pause. The Elders, while some of the oldest, were also those who had proved to have the strongest of wills. The idea that all of them had succumbed to madness at once didn't make any sense.

"What were they saying?" I asked.

"Strange muttering about The Manaha Spirit. You haven't been in The Mist, so you don't know."

Rosenthal looked away. "Something is whispering to us while we're transformed. Calling to us. Something that I fear is afflicting the Wendigo and the other Kin."

The idea struck me as absurd. We were apex predators, the alpha carnivores. Known as "Kin" internationally and as Wendigo here in the United States, we were the thing horror legends were based on. The notion that some outside force was attacking us seemed unthinkable. Unless it was another faction with the Carrion Court, which upon reflection, wasn't outside the realm of possibility.

I stood up and began pacing. "Have you heard these whisperings in The Mist?"

"Only once, briefly. I won't lie, it scared me. I transformed back quickly."

"And so, what's the theory?"

"Unfortunately, many Kin feel this is the Spirit finally communing with us."

"Bullshit."

Rosenthal took a sip. "Indeed."

"How extensive is this?"

"Without the Elders overseeing things, we don't know. But it hits closer to home."

"How do you mean?"

Rosenthal sighed. "My latest charge has gone missing. I didn't know her well, her placement into my care was requested. Holly Freemont has only been a Wendigo for about five years. She's already had a brush with The Elders due to some of her uncontrollable actions. I worry into what she's gotten into."

"You think she's gone feral?"

"I don't know, but I need new eyes on this. Eyes that I can trust. Things are getting too peculiar to not be significant."

CHAPTER 4

KELSEY

Sometimes I get a little too wrapped up in my work. What can I say? I enjoy it. I'm proud to be born a member of the Sect, and I revel in my heritage. I wouldn't want to be a member of any other Tribe, even with some of their powers and longevity, and I'd never dream of being merely human.

Of being prey.

I hadn't heard Jeff come in over the sound of Summer screaming. Her nipples had stayed intact for now, opting instead for her toes. The sound of each one coming off was like the snap of baby carrots between your teeth. It was making me hungry. Maybe that was just the baby inside me. Still, I noticed my plaything's eyes dart up to the doorway and I turned.

"Having a good time?" Jeff asked.

He asked that or a variation of that most mornings when he found me in the shack. He was short, fit, with dirty blonde hair, and blue eyes. He wasn't particularly bright, but he was absolutely devoted to me. Both of those qualities could sometimes irritate me. I suppose I wouldn't have minded his obsession so much if he hadn't been so stupid.

When I had been a child, I took IQ and aptitude tests. It seems that I scored quite high, because the state's education administrators wanted to send me to a gifted school elsewhere. Of course, my mom wouldn't hear of it. Being a young Sect, that probably would have ended badly. In high school, my grades weren't always the best, but I took a test my Junior year before I got pregnant and dropped out. Mensa, for geniuses. I passed.

"I'm having a better time than Summer here," I said, lining up four of her clipped toes in a row in the dirt.

Jeff came up behind me and slid a hand down the front of my tank top. I rarely wore a bra since I barely had B cups. He cupped my right breast and began to rub his fingers along my left nipple. I stared at Summer's nipples and fantasized about biting them off.

We had fucked in front of victims before, but I wasn't in the mood today. Besides, Summer was past the point where the act would've traumatized her, and I needed to try and induce trauma another way. I was also, going to get my dad to pick up some more straw to throw down on the floor to soak up some of this blood. It occurred to me that Jeff's erection was hitting me in the shoulder.

As I was about to say something, Tessa bounced in. She looked exactly like an eleven-year old version of me, but with light brown hair yet to discover dye. She also, hadn't bloomed into the magic yet. For some reason, she adored Jeff, and vice versa. Swearing under his breath, he quickly pulled away from me, and wandered off to study the chains on the far wall. I couldn't hide my smile.

"Hey mini-me, what's up?" I asked her.

"Dad already left, so, momma says one of you need to drive me to school."

Jeff rolled his eyes. "Can't you walk? Or Fly? Maybe you can swim there!"

"Jeff!"

They both started giggling and chasing each other around the shack. I stared at Summer, my chin in my palm. She was watching all of it unfold, aghast.

"Who are you people?" she screeched.

"We are witches, and you're gonna be dead," replied Tessa in a sing-song voice.

All I could do was laugh. "She's right, you know."

Jeff stopped besides and leaned down for a kiss. "I'll get ready now and take Tessa in before work. See you later tonight."

"Okay, baby. And you learn lots today, Tessa."

"I will," said my sister, as she was leaving the shack, turning at the last moment. "Oh, momma wants to see you. I almost forgot."

Fuck.

"I'll be right there."

I stared at the walls of the shack, they held a patina of blood and gore which was caked on thickly. The floor was becoming muddy after soaking up so much viscera. It would all be worth it. It had to be. I believed in Pith, the prophecy, and the promises.

Reaching out, I clamped my fingers tight onto Summer face and planted a kiss on her lips. She was either too surprised or too terrified to respond. I didn't want her fear in that case, it was just for me. I wondered if she had a boyfriend out there somewhere looking for her, a girlfriend? Family and friends were beside themselves in dread over her going missing, I assumed. She hadn't been gone long, but did they know they'd never see her again? Part of me was curious and wanted to ask about her life, and part of me didn't give a damn.

My fingers traced patterns in the ground, slowly working their way closer to the branch cutters. Summer began to whimper and I smiled. All she had left on the foot was her pinky toe. I caressed the tiny digit with the edge of the blade.

"Please."

"Beg louder."

"Please no, please! Please don't hurt me anymore!"

"No."

I snipped off her toe with ease and the young woman screamed. Leaning in, I inhaled deeply, and what appeared as a thick cloud of smoke issued out of her mouth and into mine. Holding it there, I climbed to my feet, and made my way over to where Ruby hung on the far wall. Her mouth had been pried open after death, a ready vessel for the fear. I billowed a majority of it inside, my lips against my dead sister, seasoning it for what was to come. So much magic, so much else was being pulled from the other corners of the Carrion Court for the grand experiment. If it worked, the bloodshed would be apocalyptic.

And it would work.

Walking back in front of Summer, I stopped long enough to pick up the toe off the ground a pop it in my mouth before heading out of the shack. She shrieked even louder.

CHAPTER 5

DANIEL

Rosenthal let me go bed down for a few hours of sleep. My old room was mostly as I had left it. Grey walls, with navy blue curtains and matching sheets, antique oak furniture. I brought up my bag and hung up my clothing in the wardrobe, thinking I might be here for longer than I had initially planned. Laying down, sleep didn't want to come. Drifting through my mind were a combination of memories and the suspicions Rosenthal had just laid on me.

The first time I had been here was in 1994. I just finished a short stint in the county jail for a B&E, which was a stupid move on my part. By that point, I was already leaning towards a life of crime; with petty theft and boosting cars on my rap sheet. I had always worked alone, but the first time I worked with a partner he'd gotten greedy and gotten us caught. On parole, and working as a line cook, I was contacted by Gerald Rosenthal one day at work.

It had been weird. I was taking a smoke break out back when he approached me. He asked me for a light. He lit his cigarette but never smoked it. Saying he knew of my skills and wanted to talk to me. That I should come see him later that day. I thought he was some kind of boss from a crime family. I borrowed a car and zipped out to the estate, thinking this was my ticket. The interview did not go as I had expected.

He asked me a lot of questions about whether I had ever thought about killing anyone, could I ever kill anyone. Sure, I'd thought about it, everybody had. I don't know if I could, but I'd never been in the position. He liked that I was an only child, that my dad had died and my mom and I no longer spoke. He also liked that I had a "questionable moral compass." I asked him exactly what kind of job he was planning and he laughed.

He took me to the back porch where he began to undress. I reacted badly, to say the least. Something in his voice when he shouted at me made me stay. It wasn't a request; it was a command. His voice had grown deeper, throatier. Still, I didn't understand was a naked man had to do with my job.

Then Rosenthal went into The Mist and transformed.

In that moment, I saw both my future and my past.

We didn't have a lot of money growing up, and while my parents tried, they both worked full time jobs to keep us fed. I often think that's why I strayed into crime, but that's for the psychoanalysts to decide. Regardless, they were either not home enough or were too tired to keep up with me. One time when I was seven years old, we had learned about shooting stars in schools. I was fascinated. The idea of stars rocketing through the sky above lit up my imagination. That night, while my dad was at work and my mom was asleep on the couch, I snuck out to hunt for shooting stars.

Now, this is seven-year-old me, so, I had everything I thought I would need in chilly March evening. My snow boots, my book bag filled with two comic books, an apple, my dad's pocketknife, an empty roll of toilet paper to act as a telescope, and a flashlight. Once I got into the woods, I retrieved the empty roll and began to peer up into the sky. Nothing. Using the flashlight, I made my way deeper into the underbrush, having no idea where I was heading.

It wasn't too cold, and I was propelled by the mission. I remember thinking that if I could find a shooting star, everything would be better. Better how, I didn't know... just better. I was so busy gazing up, I wasn't paying attention to where I was going.

I tripped and fell hard, my make-shift telescope was lost in the underbrush. Starting to complain to myself out loud, I turned and saw a hand. I had tripped over an outstretched arm. For a few moments that didn't make sense to me. Why would there be an arm out here in the woods? Then I saw the rest of a woman's body, laying there half-naked and splayed open, bloody. A scream threatened to bubble up inside my throat. Before it could come, I saw a thing rise up from out of the shadows.

It was gigantic, and far bigger than my dad. It was lean yet muscular, it had pale, albino skin with wisps of white hair blowing off in patches. Its arms were too long for a person's; its fingers longer still that ended in talons. Its face was more like that of a human skull. Having sunken eyes that held white orbs, a dual slit for a nose, and a jaw that unhinged like a snake's revealing rows of jagged teeth. From its nearly bald head sprouted two diseased-looking deer antlers. Blood splattered the entirety of the creature giving it dark brown hue in the moonlight.

I couldn't move. I couldn't breathe. The monster vanished.

The police and rescue workers found me the next day curled up next to the body in shock. Everyone assumed I had stumbled upon an animal eating the woman and concocted the fantasy in my head to explain the trauma. Her car had broken down along the side of the road a few miles away. No one ever figured out why she had ended up in the forest. It didn't matter. I was plagued by nightmares for years. I wouldn't go near the woods. I wouldn't even play outside some days. But I eventually got past it.

Until that first day on Rosenthal's back porch. Until I saw him transform. My nightmare had come back. But there was something different about it this time, something majestic. And then a voice rang out inside my head.

"You can be one, too."

CHAPTER 6

KELSEY

The main house was a large two-story affair with four bedrooms, two bathrooms, and all that. In its day, it had been a beautiful home. But, today, it was a farmhouse on the hill without a farm to overlook. My Grandma Judy's father had built it along with her brothers and sisters. She's the only one left from that generation now, left to see the place whither. The white paint has peeled and gone gray, the shutters have all but fallen off and the porch sunken into the ground where the renovated concrete foundation hasn't crumbled apart. There were more of us back then, and we were able to keep maintaining the old place. We also weren't as damaged then.

I could hear my mom as soon as I entered the house.

My face, I got from her: Angela Radu. Large dark eyes, small and pointy nose, wide mouth with cupid bow lips. People seem to think I'm attractive but all I see in my reflection is a hillbilly. All I see is my mom, who used to be curvy but now is approximately four times the size of me. She had her own brush with wild magic nearly a decade ago and it warped her mind. The excessive eating was just a byproduct of that experience.

"Everyone wants to see me dead!" screeched Angela Radu.

At the moment, I couldn't argue with her.

She reclined back on the couch straining under her weight in a stained housecoat and pawed at a bucket of cold fried chicken. Tiny bones were strewn all around her on the floor. She wiped her greasy thick fingers on the edge of the upholstery and glared at me as I entered. Obviously, in her mind, I was part of the cabal that sought her doom today. She glared, and I didn't give her the satisfaction of returning the look. Instead, I made my way over to the side of the room, under a watercolor still life of some flowers, where Grandma Judy sat in her wheelchair. The mischief in her smile was unmistakable.

I tapped my cheek and her eyes lit up. Opening her mouth and tilting back her head, I leaned over and dropped the toe from my mouth into her, like feeding a baby bird. Grandma Judy sucked on it with glee.

"That's some tasty fear," she exclaimed around the toe.

"Nothing for your poor, suffering mother?"

"You can waddle your way outside," I said. "She can't."

"Forsaken, forsaken!" wailed Angela. "Forsaken and disrespected!"

I glanced back to my grandma. "Have you eaten yet?"

"She has a good grip on that chicken."

With a sigh, I shuffled off into the kitchen. Grandma Judy didn't need to consume much fear anymore to survive, her magic dwindling in old age. She had given birth to four daughters, one dead, two had moved away to form new covens, and my mom remaining. My mom still needed as much fear as I did, but her appetite for food outmatched that, anymore. I swear most of the money dad made went into her belly. We had tried simply starving her, but she roared day and night until somebody shoved ice cream at her.

We had to find an extra refrigerator to store all the goods that were consumed by her on a regular basis. At least today, mom had her chicken to start her out with, and hadn't rummaged around making a mess. I pulled out two cartons of eggs, two packages of bacon, and a loaf of bread. We had found what looked like a flat-top griddle in the junk yard that fit perfectly over all four stoves, and we used that most days. It was easier. I turned everything on while I started toasting the bread and got a mixing bowl down to scramble up the eggs with some milk and seasonings.

It was a massive amount of food and would take over an hour to clean up afterwards. Fortunately, there was a decent amount of leftovers and mom would have no problem eating any of it cold. I wouldn't have to bother making anything for her later, hopefully. She was fully capable of attending to meals herself, and she did half the time when she wasn't in the grip of her madness. Honestly, I'm surprised she ate what I made, her paranoia convinced her that I was trying to poison her, or some nonsense.

"How's the spell coming?" asked Angela between mouthfuls.

"It's getting there," I said. "I'm definitely making progress, I can feel the vessel getting stronger, but I can't tell how long it will take."

"Ruby."

"What?"

"It's not a 'vessel,' it's your sister, Ruby."

"I know, mom. I'm in there every day with her."

She wouldn't let it go. She seemed to think that I didn't experience loss, too. Ruby had been my best friend, my idol. She was literally who I imagined that I wanted to be when I grew up. She was funny, beautiful, cool... fearless. Her death had torn my heart out. My mom made it all about herself from day one.

She had reluctantly supported the plan, mainly I suppose, because it came from Pith. She understood, in her own way, and my grandma fully backed me in the magic. Tessa was still too young and dad didn't have any magic. Secretly, I think she was more pissed that I was chosen to carry it out, that I was the new priestess of the coven.

"Did you hear me?"

I hadn't. I hadn't been paying attention to Angela Radu for years now.

"Nope. What did you say?"

"You got a job to do, little girl," she said, wagging a fat finger in my direction. "Honoring your sister and honoring Pith. I think you enjoy your time in the shack too much."

"That's the god damn point, Angela!" remarked Grandma Judy, slapping the handles of her wheelchair.

"Don't you defend her, you're supposed to side with me!"

"Your side is wrong!"

As they sat there yelling at each other, I simply got up and walked out.

CHAPTER 7

DANIEL

I actually managed to get some sleep and awoke to Rosenthal cooking. We don't always eat human flesh. We only need a steady diet of it to retain our virtual immortality. I try to get a little bit twice a month, for instance. That seems to work for me. Some Kin need more, some less. Otherwise, we eat and drink like anyone else.

Today, Rosenthal was preparing a meal of baked chicken, roasted red skinned potatoes, and fresh steamed green beans. It was a simple meal, but delicious. I had missed the old man's cooking as much as I missed Indiana. He served up the plates with some imported beers from Germany. We sat in the kitchen and ate, keeping the conversation light.

He was in an import-export business, one he had been handling in some capacity now for over sixty years. The company mostly dealt with antiques and art. Rosenthal had made his own fortune independent of the stipend granted to him by the Elders. He had always wanted me to come work for him, but I didn't know anything about his world other than maybe how to steal some of the stuff. Rosenthal didn't push the mater, but I know it disappointed him.

I had done a whole lot of nothing in the last few decades. I tried to go legit twice, by opening a bar once and trying to work as a limo driver, but both had failed spectacularly. I simply wasn't wired to operate that way, day in, day out. I needed more spontaneity, a bit more madness. These days, I didn't even take jobs for the pay off − I didn't need it. I took them for the entertainment factor.

Don't get me wrong, I'm not one of those adrenaline junkies. It's not like I fear boredom, although I do get into bouts of ennui at times. I suppose I'm simply looking for a glimmer of meaning in my life. A few brief moments of purpose. I'll find that I'm more emotionally fulfilled knocking off a bank than I ever will be if I were pushing papers at a real estate office.

After dinner we retired to the back porch. Always civilized, Rosenthal offered cigars and brandy. I puffed away, enjoying the crisp night air. No idea what brands he had given me, but knowing Rosenthal, they were expensive. The man lived a pretty reserved life all things considered, but he had his excesses.

"What more can you tell me about The Elders?" I asked.

"There's always been a faction that thought we needed to be more barbaric. Koller thinks these zealots have gained control in the wake of this uneasy time. The last few reports out were of Kin lashing out across the globe."

I was shocked by this. The whole point of being our kind was to keep hidden from the public-eye, so you could live out lifetimes. Ferals who acted only on their passion were put-down. Rampaging Kin threatened the whole system of preservation. It was especially frowned upon by The Carrion Court, but I wasn't all that familiar with them.

"So, all this is because something might be whispering in The Mist that some people think is the great Wendigo God finally talking to us?"

"That's the gist of it."

Only a certain percentage of people were looked upon by what the Wendigo called The Manaha Spirit. Only they could become Kin if they ate the flesh of another human. Otherwise you just had your average cannibal. Kin recognized Kin, even those who had not yet tasted flesh. It was why Rosenthal hadn't killed me in the woods when I was seven. Maybe it was a 'spirit,' maybe it was a genetic predisposition, I don't know. But, I knew these ghost stories I was hearing now sounded like bullshit.

"What do you honestly think?" I asked him.

Rosenthal took a sip. "Something has changed in The Mist. Were there voices? Maybe. Something moving? I don't know. I'm certainly not about to say it was the Spirit."

I set down my glass. "Fuck it, let's find out."

"What, now?"

"Yes now," I said, pulling off my shirt.

Rosenthal sighed and slipped off his shoes. "This is probably a bad idea."

*   *   *

The transformation from human into Wendigo is not like what you may imagine. It's not the painful process portrayed in werewolf movies. Once stripped naked, The Mist comes, fast and billows seemingly out of nowhere. It envelops us, and our bodies become more like a gel. We re-shape, taking on the properties of our new form. The Mist adds some mass to our flesh, as well.. It doesn't take long, maybe a minute or two. It can go faster if we force it, but there is pain then. We emerge as something grander, something stronger.

Our mouths are no longer built for speaking, only to devour, but we can communicate via short-range telepathy. This works among other Kin as well as humans. Nothing needed to be said tonight, The Mist still curling around our legs as we leapt into the tree line. We ran for miles, as kings of the earth, with no purpose tonight other than to be majestic.

Majestic and horrifying. Our forms are tall, seven to eight feet, with pale gray skin. We're covered in wisps or hair that tend to be reminiscent of our own natural hair. Our limbs are elongated out of proportion to our torso, our legs become digitigrade like a dogs' or horse. Claws more like talons from both feet and hands. Ears develop large and bat-like, noses turn up into something like a small snout, and our eyes become enlarged and strangely white. Finally, and perhaps the most bizarre to conceptualize, we develop a set of horns that are more akin to deer antlers.

The moon gleamed in the darkness. I cut my way through the night, a being free and pure in purpose. Move faster, kill surer. No shark or tiger was as great a living threat as a Wendigo on the hunt. We hear pine needles fall from trees, saw insects jump in the underbrush, caught the scent of a rotting animal over two miles away. The forest was ours, we had dominion over every rock and every blade of grass.

I ran faster and leapt over a group of low bushes. The air smelled clean and alive, back in Miami, there was no comparable scent. Stars twinkled above, though none were shooting tonight. Although I had just eaten, I wanted someone to hunt for the sport of it, the thrill of it. I wanted to hear them thrashing through the woods in terror as they tried to escape me, the smell of fear in their sweat. The little noises they made, like the bleating of a sheep. The Mist swirled around me, and I became excited for the hunt.

At first, I thought it was in The Mist, until something shifted in my peripheral vision. I turned looking, but there was nothing. Then it happened again. I stumbled, looking for what was moving among the trees that my other senses couldn't make out. I called for Rosenthal, but he was too far way to hear my thoughts.

Shadows coalesced. Light became harsh in spots and suddenly a high contrast glare obscured my ability to make out shapes. There were no longer any scents of the woods. An indistinct buzzing filled my ears, something akin to perhaps mumbling. It had no source and came at me from all sides. From inside my head, perhaps. My clawed hands came up to cover my pointed ears, trying to hold out the sound that grew louder. Grew into a roar. A voice I hadn't heard before spoke with a booming familiarity that pierced through the softer mumbling...

...My Child...

I fell back into a shallow ravine, transforming back into a human form as I went. I landed on a bed of moss which took the brunt of my fall. I lay there for a moment staring up at the canopy of leaves.

I had only been a Wendigo for a little over twenty years, but I felt like I understood what it meant to be one. The ethos of it. I didn't know what I had just experienced, but I felt confident that the voice wasn't The Manaha Spirit. It lacked the Animus. It was too empty, too hollow. The Kin were ferociously alive, an embodiment of carnivorous essence. Some theorized we were the link in between man and the environment itself. No, whatever that was, it wasn't our Spirit, it lacked the equilibrium with nature that we had.

Climbing to my feet, I began calling out for Rosenthal. It took a few minutes, but I finally found him staggering towards me. He looked about as battered as I felt.

"Did you hear it?" he asked, weakly.

"Yeah, I heard it."

"It was worse than before."

"I don't know what the hell that was, but..."

"... it's not the Manaha Spirit," Rosenthal finished for me.

"Glad we're on the same page."

"Let's get back home, this has been a terribly illuminating night."

CHAPTER 8

KELSEY

J eff wanted me to quit smoking when we found out I was pregnant. I told him that I would just to shut him up, but it was sort of a lie. I had cigarettes stashed all over the place and smoked them as I needed them. I found I still needed a couple every day. I didn't want to smoke with my daughter coming, but it was harder than he apparently thought it was to quit.

I sat on this large rock we could never move behind the trailer and lit up. Staring off into the woods, I exhaled and thought of growing up on the hill in Ennis, Ohio. It was a small, shitty town, and I had always been at the lower-class end. My family was White Trash. Kids had made fun at me at school for a variety of reasons. Meredith Gains made fun of the holes in my shoes once in fifth grade and I broke her nose. Living up to the standard and confirming stereotype of having a propensity for drama. Later I learned to use magic and do things in a subtler fashion.

I need a good dose of fear to cast, but I have innate skills over the mind. I've got the ability to create illusions, make people fall asleep, hold them in in a temporary paralysis, cause someone to become violently ill, and scry a person's location. I could do all that when I was about fourteen and I'm seventeen now, I've grown since then. Meredith Gains never got over shitting herself in the lunchroom freshman year, but that's what you get when you cross a Witch.

There are members of the Sect that can do astounding things, who have abilities that liken to that of the Throng or the Vacant. I don't have that many powers, but the powers I do have are unnaturally strong for someone my age. I'm guessing that's one of the reasons I was picked by Pith. That, and I had a dead sister lying around.

See, the Tribes have become stagnant... held in complacency by the Carrion Court. It's time the humans know true fear. If enough fear is gathered up and placed into the vessel, into Ruby, it will be primed for Pith to enter it. The God of the Sect will become manifest upon the earth and walk, no longer imprisoned in the Outer Realms. Even now, Pith draws near, feeding and disrupting the energies of his fellow Carrion gods. It's my understanding the Kin will be particularly unsettled.

This wasn't a secret. Many other members of the Sect were aware of what was transpiring here, and they had carefully chosen to feign ignorance. If it worked, they could celebrate, and if it failed, they could claim they were never aware of my transgressions. They were cowards, all of them. I think some of the male Sect members were especially put off by the fact that a teenage girl had been Pith's choice for this duty. Hey, our bloodline had always been women as far back as Court records show and we were just as worthy. I'm sorry that your fragile masculinity couldn't handle that.

The cigarette helped calm me down after the display from my mom in the house. They would never understand. Sure, I was doing this for Pith and for Ruby, but I was doing this for me. I wanted out of here. Sure, having power would be great, but I didn't want to spend my whole life on the hill. My family couldn't think any bigger than that, and Jeff didn't want any more than that. I couldn't put into words exactly what it was that I did want, what life I dreamed of... But, it was simply more than this. My life here was too small, too mundane.

Sometimes I thought about leaving. Packing a few of my things, taking one of the cars, and bailing out. My dad would be sad, but I think he would understand. So would Grandma Judy. I honestly didn't care about my mom. Jeff would lose his mind and try to find me, but I could evade him. Like I said, he's not that smart. In the end, I stayed for Tessa. She needed me. I know I should've put myself and the baby first, but I felt like my sister would suffer without me. And, anyhow: now I had this mission from Pith, so it hopefully it would all work out.

The experience in talking to Pith surpassed the pleasure from any spell casting I had ever done. It was better than an orgasm, better than extracting fear. I was truly touching the divine. My family worshipped, though the Sect god only spoke to me. They had no idea. I wish I could engage with Pith more often, but there was a risk that the other Carrion Gods might discover what we were up to.

That worried me more than the cops – other Tribes. Sect had become proficient over decades in their methods with abduction and murder so, I wasn't concerned with the local authorities tracking us down. No, it was that the Kin or Vacant might catch wind of what I was up to. I had never met another Tribe member, but I'd heard stories from Grandma Judy. The idea of a gang of Vacant, three pissed off Djinn, appearing outside the shack looking for answers didn't appeal to me.

Cigarette finished, I stamped it out on the rock and dropped the butt into an old coffee can. There were all types of junk back here, an overflow from the sheds and garages. Car parts, a broken sink, old shoes, a bag of junk mail, wet cardboard boxes, a CD player, a bicycle, and for some reason, a cash register. Utter trash, right behind my trailer in a pile.

I can remember clearly thinking, maybe I'll ask Pith to burn the whole world away, just to rid myself of the mess.

CHAPTER 9

DANIEL

The next day, I got up early for me, at noon, and began to look over everything Rosenthal had compiled on Holly Freemont. Her family, friends, hangouts, financials, a complete dossier. I was actually surprisingly good with these types of things, although I was more used to doing it to prepare for a heist. Even still, assembling data was a skill I had. Sifting through the information, however, didn't lead me to much of anything new. She had a mother back on the west coast she hadn't spoken to in years, and only a smattering of acquaintances that Rosenthal was aware of. A few minor hangouts, and meager finances. The Elders hadn't given her a stipend yet.

More troubling was the statistic that listed all the people that had gone missing or had been found brutally slaughtered in Opal and the surrounding counties in the past three months since Holly vanished. A coincidence? It was an alarming number coming in at over two dozen and I wondered how Rosenthal had gotten his hands on the report. The FBI would soon be called in to manage the caseload if they hadn't been called already. This was exactly what The Elders warned us against, if indeed Holly was behind any of that body count. Reckless behavior got you put down like a rabid dog.

I was going to have to be careful in Opal. People might actually remember me, even though it had been twenty-some years. I had been back to see Rosenthal a few times, but only for a few days, and I had never gone into town. Back then I had longish hair and was clean shaven. Now I had a fashionable five o'clock shadow. Still, it was safer to move around a little more incognito.

It took me a while rooting around through his three bathrooms, but I found a pair of hair clippers. Stripping down to my boxers, I shaved my head down to a dark stubble that matched my face. I cleaned up and stared at myself in the mirror.

I barely recognized myself, so I was hoping no one else would. At least the scruff made me look older.

✳   ✳   ✳

It seemed Holly spent a lot of time at a place called Zep's Bar. I dressed in jeans, a grey V-neck tee, and a plain black jacket, hoping it would make me inconspicuous enough. I wasn't sure where Rosenthal had gotten to, but I left him a note on a sticky pad, attached to the front of the refrigerator. Pulling away from the house I let the sounds of Cryptex take me into Opal.

Zep's didn't exist when I had previously lived in town, so it took me a while to find it. The bar had a different name all those years ago, it turned out. Parking in front of the place, it looked like the same shithole as it had been when it was called Town Tavern, back in my day. Faded reddish-brown siding, grimy windows, sidewalk littered with trash. The only thing that even gave a hint Zep's was open for business were the neon signs lit up.

It was still early, four pm now after looking over the Holly-files and getting ready, but it was worth a chance hitting the bar before it might get busy later. As soon as I opened the door, I was hit with the stench of stale beer. The place was narrow and long, darkly lit. A bunch of mirrors hung along the wall in a poor attempt to make the space look bigger. The booths had cracked, fading brown upholstery and the Formica that looked like it belonged in the 1970's. The bar itself was little better, scratches and wear marks all along the edge of the wood. All the metal barstools looked dented, likely from being wielded in fights. Some inane country song played and I gritted my teeth as I took another step inside.

There were only two patrons inside, sitting down at the end of the bar. Older men, probably in their sixties, they mumbled to each other and sipped on their beers. A middle-aged woman with tattoos wiped down the bar and didn't even glance in my direction. I didn't recognize her and hoped she wouldn't do the same for me.

"Excuse me," I said, walking up to the bar.

"Whaddya want?"

"I'm looking for Holly Freemont? Have you seen her recently?"

The bartender snorted and looked up with me. "Whaddya want with her?"

"Family friend," I lied. "I'm in town, know she hangs out here."

"Haven't seen her in forever."

"Okay, well what about..."

"Listen buddy, I'm not running a dating service," she replied as she went back to wiping down the same spot on the bar.

"Thanks for your time," I said.

She was no help. Probably didn't care one way or another. I would have to stop back later and risk more customers, ask some of them.

I went across town to Holly's apartment. She could have lived at Rosenthal's rent free, but she refused. According to him, she said she felt like she was in a cage there. Overall, she resented him and being placed in his charge by the Elders. She didn't seem to understand that it was for her own safety and that her own actions had resulted in the politely disciplinary consequences. Instead she bristled under his tutelage and ignored his mentoring. She seemed to have lashed out in any little way that she could. She got a job at a grocery store, one that paid enough for a studio apartment and booze at Zep's. She had stopped showing up at her job around the same time she had disappeared off Rosenthal's radar.

Holly's apartment was in a converted house, a half-assed renovation that the owner would do to get more rental money than if they sold the property out-right.. The whole structure looked ready to fall apart. Cheap green siding that looked more plastic that vinyl and some kind of tin roof that likely dated back before the 1940's, with large patches of rust. I took the steps on the side, simply guessing at which was her apartment since only half of the places were numbered. This was one of those times being a professional criminal came in handy, I had the lock to her door picked in under thirty seconds.

It was definitely the home of a young woman; I could tell that in one glance. The clothes, the tchotchkes, the makeup all strewn around. Making my way in, I started looking around. I found some mail and confirmed it was her place. I was actually surprised her stuff was still here, that a landlord hadn't removed it all yet. Who knows, maybe the cops had already talked to the landlord and told him Holly was part of an open investigation, the larger group of missing persons, no doubt. I swore at myself for not thinking ahead and bringing gloves. My prints were already on the door. Sloppy.

Carefully, I rooted around in her stuff for any clue one way or another. She had a lot of empty vodka bottles strewn about the place. No computer, but a charger. Police probably snagged that. Work clothes, sexy clothes, comfy clothes. That was all normal. Some self-help books, stuff on achieving your potential and maximizing your happiness. Too many self-help books could be a problem. Especially with the eighth empty vodka bottle I had found.

I sat on the bed and thought about it. There hadn't been any police tape on the door, so maybe they hadn't locked up her apartment as a crime scene. I hadn't found her computer, but I also hadn't found her wallet. Was it in a purse laying around? She could have had another charger for the computer. Maybe she just bailed, away from Rosenthal and way from the Elders. She was obviously depressed.

It was all so vague. I needed more information. Leaving the apartment, I locked up and went back to my car. Checking my notes, I saw that it said she had one good friend in town. The name sounded familiar. I didn't know how Rosenthal had deduced all this information, but I would look into all of it for him. I owed him that much.

I had no idea at the time that I was being watched.

INTERLUDE 1

Summer Holbrooke had a life before she met Kelsey Radu. She had been a twenty-three-year-old senior at The Ohio State University, getting her degree in Early Childhood Education. After discussing it with her parents, she had decided to put off getting her Masters in Child Psychology for a few years and get some work experience. They knew there weren't many jobs for their daughter in Ennis, but Mark and Maggie Holbrooke were proud of what she had achieved.

Summer had a good group of friends she socialized with regularly and an ex-boyfriend she had broken up with almost nine months ago. Dustin Mays's drinking had taken priority over their relationship and she had ended it. Dustin hadn't cared much, and he was eyeing sorority girls who led a more appealing lifestyle to his tastes. Another server at the restaurant she worked at, Fromen's Grill, had shown interest in her, but Summer had politely refused a date from Logan King. According to her, she was concentrating on her future, and at the moment it didn't involve a relationship.

She jogged a half mile every day in the morning, didn't smoke, never used drugs, and only drank socially. She listened to radio pop music, had a fondness for small dogs and children, and hated horror movies. She volunteered at the local Angels for Animals no-kill shelter four times a year during the adoption drives and had a falling out with a former best friend from high school over a boy.

All of this was known because Detective John Hayward knew it and kept going over it with his partner, Jarred Kenyon. They had just left the Ennis residence again, hoping to find one more clue, one more crumb of information that could lead them to the whereabouts of Summer. Nothing. Her parents had clutched onto each other in tears, their daughter gone for nearly a week and the police with zero to show for their efforts.

Just like the other sixteen missing people.

If this had been an isolated incident, Hayward would have assumed the young woman had bounced down to Mexico with a gaggle of girls to drink for a few days and lost track of time. It happened all the time. Most missing people weren't really missing. The last few months had been different.

"What do you think?" asked Kenyon.

"She fits the pattern," replied Hayward. "Our perp likes all types, but he prefers young women."

Out of the now-confirmed seventeen missing persons cases they were handling, four were older men, two younger men, three older women, one little boy, and seven younger women. Those women had been between the ages of sixteen to twenty-four, all relatively attractive, judging from earlier photographs if their faces were mangled. In the case of the boy, he had been abducted along with his mother and father. An entire family that had utterly vanished on their way out of town to visit the grandparents.

"This is getting out of control," said Kenyon. "McVay isn't going to let us keep on this case much longer. The FBI is going to be called in soon."

Hayward frowned. He respected the chief, but this was their case. In a town as small as Ennis, each Detective usually worked their own cases. Hell, they still wore uniforms instead of plain clothes. It was only last month when the department realized that all these missing persons were linked, that they partnered the two detectives up. Both Hayward and Kenyon were fine with that. Each at forty-two years old, they had not only come up through the academy together but graduated from Ennis Local High School the same year.

Hayward was the hothead with the good looks, prone to outbursts of temper or laughter, depending on the moment. The case had been getting to him, but he found having Kenyon there helped. While Kenyon looked like the stereotypical cop, barrel-chested and shaved head, he was far more reserved and almost Zen-like with his mischievous quips. They made great partners, except for the fact that all of Ennis was beginning to realize that the two detectives were harbingers of tragedy.

"FBI can't take this, this is ours. Besides, we don't know how all seventeen are related yet," said Hayward.

"Because gee, fourteen isn't a lot."

Hayward rolled his eyes. "You know what I'm saying."

Two years ago, the Ennis City Police Department got a grant to update all of their cruisers. Sitting in the piedmont of Appalachia, they had elected to go for durability over speed, outfitting Ford Explorers as the new vehicles. Hayward laid an elbow on the hood and put in a dip of tobacco. His wife thought he had quit, but on days like this he needed it.

"What if there's more than one perp?"

Kenyon raised an eyebrow. "That be weird, but it's possible."

"Yeah?" spitting into the ground.

"You know, it would explain some things."

"We never found the Patel van."

The Patels had been the family that went missing. Technically they weren't on the list, but everyone in the department considered them unofficial. There were three other cars unaccounted for from the cases. It would be difficult to move a stolen car and control a victim, let alone three. There were APB's out on all the cars, but not a peep.

Hayward's radio chirped. "Dispatch to Seventy-Nine, are you and Eighty-One together?"

"Ten-four," he replied.

"Situation on Sixth and Dresden, need you both on a 10-43A. 10-57 for officer on scene."

"Jesus," said Kenyon. "Shots- fired? It's that fucking trap house."

Hayward slid into the cruiser, swearing. "We have enough to worry about without junkies shooting at each other downtown."

*   *   *

The two detectives sped away to handle the incident along with their brethren on-scene. Inside, the Holbrookes continued to fret over the fate of their daughter, oblivious to her suffering and death. Oblivious to all, were the shapes in the trees, silently observing the events as they unfolded in Ennis, Ohio.

CHAPTER 10

KELSEY

Jeff was in the shack having himself a blast shattering Summer's kneecaps with a rusty ballpeen hammer I had found by one of my dad's cars. The girl wasn't screaming anymore, her pitiful sounds now more like the drawn-out mewling of a dying kitten. I suppose that comparison wasn't far off.

I had invited Jeff multiple times to enact whatever fantasies he might have upon our prey. It's not like I minded if he pleasured himself with whatever we had chained up. I certainly did. I enjoyed our victims all the time, not that he knew that. I had particular tastes. I hoped he would take on my suggestions, but he never did, said I was all he needed when it came to that sort of thing. He did like hurting them, though.

Hell, everybody likes that.

A part of me did love Jeff, kind of like the way one loves a puppy. He had followed me around since we were in elementary school. He was just another hillbilly kid from a low-rent family in Ennis, he never strove for anything in life other than a relationship with me. He stole me little trinkets in middle school to win my affection, beat up other kids who might pick on me. I might have actually loved him back for it all if he hadn't been so god damn... I don't know, normal.

He followed me to my house my freshman year on Valentine's Day with a teddy bear. He wanted to be my boyfriend, but I just wanted to rip him open and play with his intestines. My Grandma Judy cackled from the other room, offering up the idea of the shack of a good test of his devotion. Shrugging, I lead him out there. I knew my dad wasn't far behind, ready to snatch him up if he'd go off running.

I opened the door to the shack and I showed Jeff the hitchhiker we had bound and bloody on the wall. His response?

"Cool."

That was it. As a final show of allegiance to the Sect, he set fire to the hovel his family was living in, burning his mom and two sisters alive. Grandma Judy paid for the trailer we moved into on the property, much to my mom's displeasure. I still don't know if that was over the money spent or that I was technically out from under her roof.

At first, I was happy, I had someone all of my own who I could share everything with. The bliss didn't last, though. As much as I wanted him to be, Jeff wasn't the type of person I'd spent years dreaming of. I wasn't being picky; it just wasn't like that.

He wasn't a girl.

It's shitty to say that, but there it is. I used him to give me a baby. I could have perhaps gotten past the stupidity and clinginess if Jeff had a different set of genitals. Guys are fun to play with every now and again, but not for long term use. I'm willing to bet vast quantities of money, which I don't have, that Jeff had figured this detail out about me long ago but was convinced his undying love could change me or some nonsense.

Pith couldn't come soon enough.

Now Jeff strolled out of the shack, splattered with blood and huge grin spread across his face. I was sprawled in a lawn chair, soaking in what little sun there was and waiting for him. The sky always seemed to be gray in northern Ohio. He plopped down in the grass and waited for my acknowledgment like a good boy.

"She made some interesting noises," I said.

"I stayed away from vital organs, like you showed me."

"She passed out?"

"Don't think so."

"Excellent."

"Do you care if I help your dad today on something? Gonna make an extra eighty bucks moving some stuff out of a storage unit over in Schwepton."

"I don't care, hon," I said, running my hand along his face. "Be careful."

He kissed my fingers. I did love him, but not in the way that I should. It made me sad to think about, and I thought about it often. Jeff wasn't a bad guy, and he deserved someone who could give him one hundred percent. There was probably another murderous sociopath out there somewhere for him.

I got to my feet and stretched. "Okay, time for Summer to give her last. You go get ready and I'll see you later tonight."

He gave me a peck on the forehead and raced off to get cleaned up. Moseying into the shack, I glanced down at the ruin that he had left Summer in. She was barely hanging on, her breath coming in gurgling spurts. Yep, she was almost done.

Over on the bench, I picked up a mechanic's screwdriver easily ten inches long from its handle. The metal gleamed in the light, ready for use. Straddling Summer, she began to make those little cat noises again, gawking at me with her one good eye. Jeff hadn't mentioned he'd taken out her right eye. I didn't see it anywhere.

"Summer, you've been a delight, but it's time to set you free."

"Wha..."

"By free, I mean kill you."

"No, please."

I leaned in and kissed her, pulling back to peer deeply into her remaining left eye. Gripping her face, I slowly slid the screwdriver into her right ear, making sure she could feel it penetrate. Her good eye went large, larger, then the light went out of it. My lips on hers again, I sucked the last remnants of fear from her body.

Deposited into Ruby, I went to take a shower. I felt better about the day now that Summer was finished. It meant a new hunt, new toys. A better tomorrow was on its way. Feeling reinvigorated, I slipped on black yoga pants, an old My Chemical Romance shirt I had found at the thrift store, and blue flip flops.

Hopefully, Mom wouldn't piss me off today.

CHAPTER 11

DANIEL

It was another apartment, this one in a run-down tenement complex. Six stories of crumbling brown bricks only a stone's throw away from a set of train tracks. What little grass that qualified as a courtyard was off to the side of the building. The front of the parking lot was littered with beer cans, cigarette butts, and takeout food wrappers. A faded, paint chipped skeleton of a swing set sat next to a weather-beaten wood picnic table, the boards had all warped from exposure to the elements. Three guys huddled around the table and ignored me as I got out of my car. I ignored them just the same as I made my way into the building.

Emily Brower lived in 402. That name still tickled at the back of my skull. I walked up four flights of stairs, pissed at myself that I couldn't recall why it felt familiar. I hoped it wasn't someone I knew from back in the day. The hallways were as narrow as the stairwells, with dirty off-white walls and stained tile floors. The apartment was easy enough to find.

Knocking brought a shrill, "Who's there?"

"Ms. Brower?"

The door cracked open and managed to see a dumpy woman in her late forties with stringy brown hair and small, watery eyes.

"I'm looking for Emily Brower."

"Why? Who are you?"

"A mutual friend," I said. "I was hoping her and I could..."

"She's dead," the woman spat out. "Killed up there in them woods two months ago. Now leave me the hell alone."

The door slammed back in my face as it finally came back to me. Emily Brower's name had been on the list of victims I had read earlier in the day. How hadn't I recognized the same name so soon after?

That shook me. I wondered why I was so far off my game. I excelled at what I did because I was excellent at planning, at seeing all the possible angles. I did research, mapped things out. Knew all the players, all the plot points. This was twice now today that I had fumbled. I tried to chalk it up to being back in Opal, that my nerves were on edge being home. I didn't want to think about it having anything to do with what I had experienced in The Mist last night. That was a road I didn't want to think about.

I hadn't eaten all day so, I swung through the drive-thru of the nearest burger joint. I parked in the lot and ate, thinking as I munched on some fries. It was less likely that Holly took off with her only known friend coming up dead. I mean, it could be a coincidence, but that seemed farfetched to me. Not given Holly's past. I pulled out to call Rosenthal to update him, but he didn't answer. I left a voicemail telling him to call me back.

Not sure what else to do at the moment, I went to the library. It hadn't changed at all since I was last there, having been forced to do a history report for Mr. Hogue's class in 10th grade. I slid past the woman at the desk who didn't even look up at me and went upstairs. There was a solitary old woman on the bank of computers lined up against a wall, and I took one at the end.

I logged in using one of many of my fake email accounts and started looking up info about the ongoing case. Sure, I had more than what was available online back at the Rosenthal's house, but I wanted a quick glance at some things. Six dead, fifteen missing. Why were more missing than those found dead? Did that matter? The area around Opal was pretty dense with woodlands, but it wasn't like it sat inside some giant national park. For some reason I couldn't wrap my head around it.

I kept going over what little data I could pull up, trying to corroborate it with what few details I knew to be true. Eventually, I gave up and restarted the computer. It had grown later than I had imagined and the library was closing down. Nodding at the woman at desk on my way out, I figured I might as well hit Zep's one last time before I head back.

*   *   *

There were a half a dozen cars parked outside the place when I pulled up this time. That was promising. Even if the same bartender was on duty, hopefully some of the patrons might know something. It was turning eight pm, but dusk was dropping. I thought about calling Rosenthal again, but figure I wouldn't be in the bar for long either way.

Stepping inside, I tried to gauge the mood of the bar but was instantly mesmerized by a commotion over near the taps. A young woman was fighting with the bartender; the same surly lady who hadn't been much help to me earlier. She didn't seem to want to help now, either. I took a few more steps in when the bartender noticed me. She pointed in my direction. The young woman leaning over the bar left her spot there and marched over to me.

"Where's my sister?" she asked.

"Who the hell is your sister?" I asked, confused.

She was remarkably attractive, tall and slender with dark skin and long curly black hair. Wide eyes that showed all of her emotion, all of her anger. I had seen beauty of all kinds in my time, but something about her really affected me, and that almost bothered me.

"Cameron Pembroke," she replied.

"Okay, and you are?"

"Keegan Pembroke, but that doesn't really matter. You were asking about Holly Freemont."

My mind whirled. I didn't know how to answer, I wasn't prepared for this. She didn't feel right, and it wasn't just her looks. I couldn't put my finger on it. She was standing there in skinny jeans, tank top and a sweater, normal clothes, but it radiated like battle armor to me. I tried my best to play it off.

"So? I'm old friends with Holly."

"Holly has been missing for months. Holly and Cameron used to get drunk here together all the time with their friend Emily. Emily's dead, and now Cameron's been missing for a week. I came back into town to search for her, and you're the first lead I have."

Was Cameron's name on the missing list? I didn't remember it, but at this point today I'd probably screwed that up, too. It was hard to think with this Keegan girl in front of me, regardless.

"They're probably off on a beach somewhere," I said.

I turned around, ready to dismiss the whole night. Part of me just wanted to get away from this strange, beautiful young woman. I would keep tracking Holly tomorrow and see if Cameron was on the list of missing people back at Rosenthal's. If not, she most likely should be. I only made it two paces.

"You're lying," she said. "You think she's dead. Because of Holly."

I slowly turned around. "Why would you say that?"

Keegan made a face. "What the fuck is a Wendigo?"

I dragged her over to a booth and plopped her down across from me.

"Why would you say that?"

"I'm psychic, the real deal," she said with a smile. "Your name is Daniel Hale."

I stared at her.

"Certain stuff is really easy. Like, you are... wait, you're not that old."

I sighed. "You don't want to get involved in this."

"I'm already involved, I've been involved."

I leaned back in my seat and clicked my tongue. She frowned back at me expectantly. I'd never met a real psychic before, someone with legitimate powers. It was intriguing and, I'm not ashamed to admit, a bit frightening. It made me rethink the place we Kin thought we had in the pecking order. As that hit me, so did my next course of action.

"Fuck it, all my investigative avenues for today came up empty. What are you drinking?"

CHAPTER 12

KELSEY

I was wrong. Mom pissed me off immediately.

She was screaming at the television for no legitimate reason that I could discern. She was watching one of those reality TV shows, some utter garbage like "Cheated on while Seven-Hundred Pounds and Pregnant." Something on the program had offended her delicate sensibilities and now she was bellowing insults at the characters like they could hear her, the fat rolls around her neck quivering in impotent rage. This was happening too often, these exaggerated outbursts against trivial matters. The rest of the family pitied her, and I once did too. But, not anymore.

"It's a television show, mom. Calm down."

Grandma Judy chuckled.

"Such disrespect! Don't think you're too big for me to lay hands on!"

"I'd butcher you there on that couch, you babbling psychotic."

She tried to wobble up off her cushioned throne but fell back twice. I wasn't scared of her, physically or magically. In both cases, I was stronger and she knew it. I opened my mouth, looking for words to say to Grandma Judy, but nothing came. The old woman shook her head and shooed me out.

I wasn't scared of my mom, just scared of becoming her.

*　*　*

I had to get away, at least for a little bit.

There were always extra cars on the property, some we had taken from the prey. Some had their parts getting stripped down to sell at the junkyard. Instead I snagged the keys to a Pontiac Vibe that had seen better days and drove into town.

I didn't really need anything but picking up a few items would make me feel better. Like a normal person, I guess. There was a dollar store where I could pick up hair ties, another pack of smokes, some juice, and whatever else caught my eye. Jeff had no problem leaving me cash, although sometimes this led to arguments. Not about the amount, but where he got it from. The boy couldn't hold a job to save his life and tended to take odd jobs that weren't exactly legal. I didn't care as long as it didn't lead back to me, and I didn't trust him to ensure that.

As soon as I walked into the store, I saw Liz McCreary. Dear Pith, I hadn't seen her in two years, and she looked even better than before. I was a sophomore when she was been a senior. We were both at a party some jackass named Terry was throwing. Both drunk, we had ended up in the laundry room making out. She had been the first girl I had kissed and fantasized about. I had kissed a couple girls before that, but they had all been playthings in the shack. Liz had been different.

A few inches shorter than my five-six, she was curvy with porcelain skin and freckles, ginger hair, and brown eyes. About as Celtic-looking as you can get. She had this laugh that sounded like a cartoon, that made me smile every time I heard it. I thought she had gone to college out of state somewhere, but here she stood. I probably looked like an idiot gaping at her.

"Kelsey, oh my god! How have you been?"

I composed myself enough for a response, unable to take my eyes off her. She looked amazing in her skinny jeans and button-down green flannel. The shirt barely held-in her Double D breasts behind the store apron. I had spent countless hours after our tumble thinking about her, Jeff was none the wiser. He had been working the night of the party and never knew about my indiscretion.

Liz said something, but I missed it, my mind was wrapped up in picturing her naked.

"I'm sorry, what was that?"

"I said, I get a thirty-minute break here soon. Meet me out back so we can catch up?"

I nodded and wandered off into the store. I found the hair ties, juice, and some ibuprofen. Back at the counter, I totally forgot to get cigarettes, I was so flustered. I didn't see Liz anywhere, and some grumpy old lady rung me up. Stashing the stuff in my car, I glanced around but the lot was empty. Depressed, I started to open the door, when I heard a voice.

"Hey, over here!"

Liz was motioning to me from the side of the building, a small lot next to an abandoned furniture warehouse. The apron was gone, and I tried to tell myself it was my imagination that an extra button had come undone. Strolling over, she gestured to the passenger side of her SUV. I climbed in and no longer bothered to hide my smile.

"It really is great to see you," I said.

"You too," said Liz.

"Thought you were off at college."

"I partied too much; my grades slipped. Age old story."

"Sorry."

"I'll miss the parties, not the school."

I sighed. "I miss the parties now."

"We were at a good one."

I can't even imagine my face at that point. "Yeah, we were."

"That was a big night for me. I figured out a lot about myself."

"Oh yeah?"

"Yeah."

And I was kissing Liz McCreary again.

This time, however, it was more than kissing and some grouping. Clothing began to peel off, hands and mouths everywhere. She looked even better than I expected her to. Wonderfully smooth, tasting like candy. This, this is what I desired.

Then she pulled my yoga pants off.

"Are you pregnant?"

I was a deer in headlights.

"It's okay, I've never fucked a pregnant chick before."

Looking back, I don't know why, but it all crumbled in. Jeff's obsession, my mom's madness, Ruby's death, upcoming motherhood, the mission for Pith. One of those moments I had been waiting for pretty much my whole life was right in from of me, and I blinked. Worse, I blamed Liz.

"Fuck you, Liz," I barked, climbing out of the vehicle, still topless.

"Wait, I don't understand!"

I stormed back to my car and threw it in reverse, squealing out of the parking lot. I still didn't have my shirt on. I could get cigarettes tomorrow, from somewhere else. I wouldn't be going back there, not ever. That's what I told myself and I flew down the road.

I made sure not to start crying until I was a good mile away from the store.

CHAPTER 13

DANIEL

I had finished my fourth beer and Keegan was still nursing her second by the time I was done telling my story. A little bit of foam left in my glass, a reminder of the domestic hefeweizen I had just drank down. She was drinking some microbrew IPA but didn't seem to be enjoying it much. Chances were it was the tale I had laid out for her and not the beer. She wouldn't look me in the eyes.

"Are you going to kill me now?" she asked quietly?

"What? No! I mean, I'm supposed to, but I don't really follow the rules as often as I should. Besides, you're some kind of unique creature – like me. Also, I feel the rules are suspended in the face of a mutually opposing enemy. At least I'm making that stipulation up right now on the fly."

She nodded, still not looking at him. "How many people have you eaten?"

I took the question with a sigh. It's a question you always expect although you rarely get asked it, since you never actually leave anyone alive to get the chance. "Keegan, I'm an apex predator. I could conceivably live for five hundred years. I eat when I have to, but I don't make a glutton of myself. I also don't count."

"I guess I can see that."

"Do you feel bad when you invade people's minds?"

"That's different!"

"Is it? Or is it us being the different types of superior beings we were designed to be?"

"Oh my god, Danny Hale!"

I looked over to see an overweight woman with blonde frizzy hair bearing down on me. She was obviously drunk, her bright red lipstick smudged. She looked vaguely familiar, but I couldn't place her at all. The woman fluttered her eyes in a horrid attempt at flirtation.

"That you Danny Hale, lookin' all good? Where you been? We been missin' you!"

I must have had a look on my face of desperation, or Keegan read it in my mind blaring like an alarm, because she stepped up.

"I'm sorry, this is my boyfriend, James."

The woman looked me over and wobbled back, her brain processing the information. It took her a few seconds, but it finally decided to click.

"Sorry, I thought you was somebody else."

I watched her meander back to the bar, grateful that I didn't have to extract myself from that situation. It would have been one thing if I had actually remembered who the hell she was, but I had no clue. That made it a lot harder.

"Thank you," I said, turning back to Keegan.

"You looked truly pathetic, had to help."

"I can't really come home, I don't age."

She laughed. "Oh, my heart breaks for you."

I smiled. I couldn't help but like her. I had felt an instant attraction and it wasn't simply because she was gorgeous. Was it because she was psychic? I didn't know, and most of me really didn't care. I noticed her blushing and realized she had probably read my thoughts. Oh well, I was glad she knew.

"So, what know?" Keegan asked.

"Now I walk you out to your car like a gentleman, then I go home and try to figure out my next step for tomorrow."

"With me."

"Okay, with you."

We got up to leave, and I paid my tab discreetly at the end of the bar. I was hoping the blonde woman would be so drunk with her friends that she wouldn't notice us leave. I wasn't paying enough attention to the rest of people in the bar, didn't even register the guy walking past us and out the door. Honestly, as we exited, I was too busy watching Keegan's ass to even check my surroundings. Another dumb move in a string of them that day.

The parking lot was little more than a gravel strip with inadequate lighting filled with vehicles parked haphazardly. It sat perpendicular along with the bar off to the road. We walked out, Keegan walking beside me. She smiled up at me in a nervous fashion. I could tell she still couldn't tell if she could trust me or not. It was to be expected, but I wanted to reassure her, let her know in some way that I would never hurt her. She may not be Kin, a Wendigo like me, but she was something else special. She pointed at a little hatchback packed near the end and we made our way towards it. If my mind hadn't been so wrapped up in her, I would have sensed the other man rushing towards us.

He had his arm around Keegan before I could stop him, a gun pressed against her ribs. Tall and slender, a white guy with disheveled brown hair and an unkempt short beard. He was the man who had pushed past me in the bar.

"Get in the red truck," tossing a set of keys onto the gravel.

I gave him a death stare, one that would rattle almost anyone, but it didn't faze him.

"The gun may not hurt you much, Hale, but it will her. Let's go."

He knew me? Knew what I was? Slowly, I reached down and retrieved the keys, never taking my eyes off of him. We all climbed into the truck, me behind the wheel, Keegan in middle, and the man in the passenger seat with the gun still pressed into Keegan. He didn't seem to like to be near her.

"Where are we going?" I asked.

"Remember where Little Chip Camp used to be?"

"That campground for kids with a cartoon chipmunk for a mascot, yeah?"

"That's where we're going. Don't try anything either. You and I would both survive, but she likely wouldn't, whatever she is."

CHAPTER 14

KELSEY

I pushed all the rage, and hate, and sadness into a little ball and hid it somewhere inside myself. It would likely fester and come out roaring at a later date, but I needed to compartmentalize it for now. I could have a meltdown later alone, after Jeff was asleep. For now, he was back with my dad, and my mom had cooked diner.

She was having a lucid period, the magic that fried her brain subsided temporarily every once in a while. I'd take what little miracles I could get. I think we all felt that way.

While my dad wasn't a Sect, he had been raised by a large coven that employed humans as servants. His childhood had been spent attending to the coven, cleaning their mansion, serving their food, sexually gratifying them. Almost thirty years ago, Grandma Judy, my mom, and her sisters had visited the coven for a Sect meeting. Teenage Angela Beaumont had been quite taken with the young Mike Radu. My dad was more or less bought as a present for my mom, but Grandma Judy never saw him as a slave.

Unlike any forced allegiance he may have had to his former coven, Mike Radu loved Angela Beaumont from their first meeting. My mom was beautiful, brash, and willing to share her life with a human. My dad proved himself to be a capable and devoted husband every single day, something the Beaumont clan came to respect. It's what Jeff attempted in his own clumsy way.

Even now, with the madness and verbal abuse, changes both mentally and physically, Mike Radu still loved his wife. It baffled me, but it made me admire him all the more. It also made me feel that much more inadequate in my contributions to our family.

The smells that wafted over me as I entered the house was amazing. The table was near overflowing with food. Salted greens cooked with ham hock, chopped cabbage stewed in broth, baked potatoes served with seasoning and sour cream, buttered noodles, and roasted pork loin with garlic and onions. Mom must've been cooking since I left, Grandma Judy was unable to do any of this from her wheelchair. She hadn't prepared a feast like this in almost two years.

"Mom, this... this looks fantastic," I said, the awe in my voice apparent.

"Take a seat, hon," she said. "You want iced tea or milk?"

"Milk, please." I heard my response but didn't believe it.

I could see the clarity in her eyes, and also, the sadness. She knew what had been happening, and while she had a grip on her life, she was going to make it count. It was right there in the way her jaw was clenched; she knew the lunacy could dance back in at any second.

We all sat down and passed around the serving dishes, filling our plates with food. The greens were exactly how I liked them; the noodles melted in my mouth. That pork loin wouldn't have tasted any better from a five-star restaurant in some city I had never been to. Jeff made a joke about getting fat, and mom quipped she already was. Dad admonished her, saying she was beautiful. No one noticed me tear up when she blushed at my dad's words.

I had to keep it together.

Grandma Judy asked us about our day. Dad and Jeff filled in everybody on their adventure cleaning out a storage unit. It had been uneventful, but they made some cash from the guy who owned the units. Tessa told us about school, and how they were learning about Europe. Grandma Judy offered to tell her some stories about our ancestors later that night, and my sister was excited. Leaving out Liz, I updated everybody on the situation in the shack and mentioned I had gone into town for a few supplies.

My dad raised a fork of potatoes to his mouth and paused. "We need to go on a hunt tonight."

"Tonight, or tomorrow."

"I'm game tonight," said Jeff.

"Can I come?" asked Tessa.

The table went silent.

"Well, I suppose that..." began my dad.

"No," said mom.

"Angela," he said. "She has to know the trade at some point."

"No!" screamed my mom, banging her fists on the table.

We all sat there, waiting for whatever came next.

Slowly, carefully, she brushed her hair back and smiled politely. "Tessa has more than enough time to learn what will be expected of her. The magic isn't even upon her yet. Let's give her a chance to be a child."

"Okay, baby," said my dad. "Not a problem."

Tessa was eleven and I was hunting at eight, but I knew why my mom was reacting this way and I didn't necessarily think it was insanity. Her eldest daughter was dead from the wild magic and her middle daughter was a pregnant high school dropout who was currently on a mission for an eldritch god. Maybe it was my own burgeoning motherly instincts, but I got it.

"Mom," I said.

Her head snapped over to gawk at me, teetering on the verge of slipping back into her natural state of frenzy.

"Thank you for dinner, the food was wonderful."

And like that, the storm passed. The tension cleared and she sighed. Reaching across the table, she took my hand.

"Thank you, KeeKee."

She hadn't called me that in years.

We all helped clear the table and put away the leftovers, Tessa began helping Jeff do the dishes. There was laughing and joking the whole time, everyone was happy. For a short time, I was happy.

Outside on the porch, dad put his arm around me.

"Thank you," he said.

I knew what he meant.

With a nod, I simply replied, "Let's go kidnap somebody."

CHAPTER 15

DANIEL

It took me a few minutes to remember the way to Little Chip Campground. It had been decades since I went driving around Opal, and for some reason I wasn't performing my best over the last two days. Part of me worried it had something to do with what I had heard in The Mist. Could it have affected me in some way already? My memory was usually sharper than this.

I took a left onto Oak St. and hoped it would buy me some time, but a vague recollection of the camp's location came back to me. Swinging another left, I took the truck out of town and head into Opal Township. Sitting in the confines of the cab, I could sense the stranger now. Keegan's presence had been overwhelming me outside of the bar, but now in such close proximity, I knew he was like me. He was Kin.

"So, is there a reason for this abduction I should be aware of?" I asked.

"Don't talk," he said. "We'll be there soon enough."

Opal Township was basically a suburb of Opal itself, but even smaller and more sparsely populated. A lot of family farms, machinery shops, local dairy ranches, and fields of nothing but grass. We zipped down one of the state routes that cut directly through the area, then turned off into a more heavily wooded section. A few more houses and an auto shop. Another turn, and the road changed to dirt. It had been graveled once, a sign hung above, welcoming children to the camp.

The trail meandered a bit before leading us to the lodge. It was a large A-Frame, almost thirty feet in height, narrow at maybe forty feet but easily over hundred feet long. Build from planks of wood in a log cabin style, it had been a marvel to me as a child. Not so much now. From behind the windshield, I could see that a fire burnt inside through the windows. As we pulled up, a woman walked out onto the porch. She was naked and covered in blood.

It was Holly Freemont.

"Get out," said the other wendigo, pulling Keegan from the truck.

I did as he asked and stepped out into the night air in front of Holly.

"Who's this bitch, Cole?" she asked.

Cole pushed Keegan forward. I moved towards them, but he waved the gun.

Holly snarled and stepped back. "What the fuck are you?"

Keegan didn't say anything. Holly's hair was in tangles, blood spattered and streaked all over her tan skin. The terrified girl either didn't notice she was naked or didn't care. I figured it was the latter. Keegan was too scared to even look up, so, I responded.

"That's Keegan Pembroke, sister of Cameron," I said, going for honesty. "She found out I was looking for you and got into my business. The general consensus is you went and ate Cameron. Not that I necessarily care about that. I was about to eat her when your thug came and swooped us up. He thought by threatening her I'd play along, but I realized it was the quickest way to finally find you."

Hoping Keegan would "hear" me, I thought very hard, *Play Along!*

Holly looked back and forth between us. "So, you don't know what she is?"

"Hot? Probably delicious? I don't know."

"Keegan Pembroke, huh," said Holly with a smile. "Cameron has talked about you. Wanna see what's happened to your sister?"

Keegan's eyes went wide, but she followed Holly inside. I went as well, Cole trailing behind me looking bored. The stench of rotting meat was bad even before the doors opened; it smelled so foul, it almost made me sick.

The giant stone fireplaces crackled at both ends of the lodge, illuminating enough of the space to show it had become an abattoir. Bodies and viscera lay strewn everywhere, some were dismembered and mutilated. A pile of arms sat in the center of the room, all with chunks bitten out. Easily accessed snacks. Heads with most of their flesh stripped away by inhuman teeth, the skulls cracked open and brains slurped out. Intestines were strung up on a chandelier along with bones tied to an old electrical cord, all like some psychotic decoration. A severed penis lay at my foot, an element of randomness from the chaos— such a pitiful thing, and a waste. Its original owner had been well-endowed.

"Cameron?" exclaimed Keegan.

Her voice interrupted a threesome in progress, the participants all naked, all Kin. A young black man sat on one of the benches while a young white woman straddled him, taking every inch between her legs. At the same time, she had an elder gentleman in her mouth. They all spun around at the sound of Keegan's voice.

"Mother fuck!" swore Cameron, pushing herself off both men, and storming over.

"I thought she was your sister?" I whispered to Keegan.

"Step-sister," she replied. "Since we were both, like, ten."

"What the hell are you doing here you little... whoa!" Cameron staggered back like she'd been slapped.

"You feel it, too?" asked Holly.

"Yeah, what's wrong with her?"

"I was going to ask you," replied Holly.

Cameron spun on Keegan. "Alright, 'Golden Girl,' what did you do? Besides trying to ruin my life in some brand-new way?"

Tears started to come from Keegan. "I would never try to ruin your life! You're my sister, my best friend! I love you!"

"Bullshit. Best grades, best boyfriends, best daughter. I always got table scraps, and you know it. Well, you can't take this from me, you're not good enough to be what I am this time. I don't know what kind of freak you are now."

Keegan began sobbing and it took every ounce of willpower I had not to comfort her. I sent out as many positive thoughts as I could, promising her I find us a way out of there. I hoped she was listening.

"This little family reunion is adorable and all, but why am I here? I assume it's because I was investigating your disappearance?"

"Oh, pretty and smart," cooed Holly.

"Seriously though?"

"I'm not going back to Rosenthal."

"Okay."

"Okay? That easy, huh?"

"I wasn't contracted to bring you in, I was contracted to find you," I said, getting creative. "Rosenthal has to have told you about me. Daniel Hale? I'm one of his biggest disappointments. I've been a career criminal my entire life, before and after The Mist. I'm the disposable one for a gig like this."

Holly gave me a sideways smile. "Hale, you're his favorite thing in the world."

I must have had a genuine look of shock on my face because she started laughing. I didn't know if I believed her or she was trying to rattle me. I blew it off and kept going.

"Regardless, I don't know what's all going on here, and I don't have to know. Now, if you..."

"Manaha."

"What?"

"Manaha, the great god of the Kin, speaks to us now in The Mist. Have you been in The Mist recently, have you heard his Voice? He tells us to shed our humanity, to give in to the monster that we spend so much time suppressing."

"To go feral?"

"To feast, to fuck, to run without fear. To be the greatest predator the planet has ever seen. To Be as we should Be."

"Um..."

"That's why I brought all of them into The Mist," said Holly, gesturing around at the others. "Every Wendigo I find will be initiated into the new will of Manaha. No more oppression, no more lessons, only terror and flesh. We will slaughter as many humans as our god wishes."

CHAPTER 16

KELSEY

The highway rest stop about thirty miles out from Ennis was a great place to hunt. The authorities never pinpointed the spot as a crime scene, and there was always a rotating cast of characters to choose from. We couldn't use it too often, or eventually someone would piece it all together, but it was one of my favorite places to play. This rest stop was so small it didn't have a night attendant, or CCTV. It was like they were asking for it.

We had snagged two girls from there in the past, plus an entire family once. Grabbing a whole family was a fascinating change of pace. Their fear had been more psychological as they had been forced to watch me torment one after another. Honestly, the little boy hadn't produced as much as I thought he would. Maybe he hadn't fully understood what was going on. Ah, but his mother had. I haven't had anyone scream so much as that mother when I was peeling her child like an apple. Some might think I spared her the agony of killing her before the boy, but as I slid the blade into her throat, I whispered a few choice words about what I was going to do to him after she was gone. The amount of fear I received out of her dying breath was extraordinary.

And you might say: But Kelsey, you're going to be a mother, have you no empathy? I am Sect, not human. My daughter will be Sect, not human. I harbor no ill will towards humans, my beloved father is human. But Humans were placed on the earth to feed us. I know where I stand in the food chain as a predator. I can protect my daughter as a Sect, and in all truth, I would have nothing but respect for a human mother who could protect its child from me.

But most can't.

There was only one big-rig parked at the rest stop when we got there. Pulling up to the tow truck behind it, I immediately went to take care of the driver. He might have already been asleep, but it was best to be sure. I knocked on his door and waited for a response.

He opened the door and smiled down at me. "Well, Howdy!"

I was in boots, black jeans, a black tank top with silver stars, and shimmery makeup. I looked good, but non-threatening, dark enough to blend into shadows, and the cut of my shirt hid my baby bump. I wondered if I looked old enough to be in college.

My left hand touched his beefy arm, while my right rested against the side on my cheek. I puckered my lips and blew a tiny plume of magic out into his face. He scrunched up his nose and looked like he was going to sneeze in the faint gray cloud.

Along with my hand, I tilted my head to the right and said, "Dashoon."

The trucker collapsed, already snoring.

He would be out for over six hours and remember nothing. Back in the tow truck, we scooped out our pickings. There was a family already here, but there were two kids and they were both teenagers. Too much to take on, I reckoned. A solitary older man in a suit, but he looked beaten down. Chances are we wouldn't be too much fun. I often wondered what would happen if we picked up a serial killer one day. Humans killed as often as we did, just for dumber reasons. It occurred to me that a serial killer would be a blast to torture, but probably wouldn't produce a great quantity of fear.

The family had departed, as had the businessman. A car full of young men had arrived, but they all stayed in the car save for one who rushed inside. None of us could make out how many were in the SUV, but it was at least three. Again, not worth the risk. As he was coming out, a blue sedan pulled up and parked. My attention was pulled away from the SUV as the new arrivals got out.

It was a young couple. I was guessing in there mid to late twenties. He was average build with dark hair and short beard. Decent looking with tired eyes. She was built like me, slender and tall, but almost six feet. She looked like a model. Her long honey-colored hair whipped around in the night breeze. She laughed and pushed him as they took the curb up to the sidewalk.

I wanted them. I wanted her.

"Them," I said.

Jeff gave me a frown. "You sure."

"Couples produce better fear," I said.

It was a decent rationale.

My dad shrugged and opened the door, holding it for Jeff. He nodded slightly, still holding his gaze on me. I threw my hands up in the air, then pointed to the rest stop. Without a comment, he exited.

Quickly, I was across the parking lot and up the sidewalk. It was easier to catch them in the restroom. We had fashioned skeleton keys to the maintenance room situated between both the men's and the women's a few years back, a room that also had a backdoor that led outside. My dad would get the boyfriend or husband or whatever with a sedative, while I went into the women's. Jeff would take care of the doors and stand guard. After they were stashed out in the trees, we would hitch up their car to the tow truck. When it was clear, they'd be stuffed in bags and carried out, one in the trunk, one in the backseat.

Washing her hands, she smiled at me as soon as I stepped inside the women's. Her blue eyes were huge. For a moment, I faltered, standing in the doorway like an idiot. Then came the sound of a scuffle, and a cry of pain from across the alcove. No more smiles now, instead alarm on her face.

I crossed the three paces in an instant and said, "Dashoon."

CHAPTER 17

DANIEL

This was worse than I could have expected. One feral Kin was bad enough, but now I had five to deal with. On top of that, they were all uber-religious nutjobs.

"I'm all for eating some humans and having an orgy," I said with a shrug, trying to keep as relaxed as possible. "But if you cause too much of a mess, it's not some pissy Elders you'll have to deal with. Eventually the Court will step in."

"The Court?" asked Cameron.

"Shut up," snapped Holly. "It's a bullshit scare tactic, a boogeyman bedtime story they use to keep us in-line."

"Dear bloody hell. Are... are you serious? The Carrion Court is real. We're not the only monsters on this planet."

Holly stormed over to me, her face in mine. She might have been passingly attractive, but the stench of dead blood and old sweat ruined that for me. Her face twisted into a scowl, she gritted her teeth and shook her head slowly at me, like she was trying to find the words. I simply stared back passively.

"Even if the Court is real, even if they would come for us, Manaha would lead us to victory."

What could I say to that? Her devotion was so complete, so absolute, she believed she and her followers could wage war against four other tribes. Wage war and win. You could see the madness in her eyes, the utter disconnection from reality. There would be no reasoning or logic here in their little handcrafted corner of hell.

So, I nodded my head and said, "Okay."

She seemed momentarily confused by this response, but then accepted it. I had a feeling her ragtag pack reacted this way to her when she made proclamations. Alphas only had that position until someone else wrestled away dominance.

The large black man that Cameron had been riding started sliding his way over towards Keegan. "Hey, can I fuck your sister, then eat her? Not in that order."

"Fuck you, Nolan! If anyone is eating my bitch sister, it's gonna be me!"

"There is something about her," said the older white guy. "She smells like summer mornings and cinnamon tea."

"Yeah, Thomas," said Nolan, stroking himself. "Dewdrops and spice."

Holly inhaled deeply. "I'd say more like Christmas morning."

"Damn, I smell it now," said Cole.

I did too, stronger than the scent I had picked up back at the bar. While it was alluring, there was still something as unnerving as attractive about Keegan. The only one who didn't seemed to sense this was Cameron. The stepsister was getting agitated at all the attention Keegan was suddenly getting.

"No!" screamed Cameron, jumping in front of Keegan. "She's nothing special, no one important! It's probably some god damn fancy body wash."

"Cameron, why..." tried Keegan.

"I hate you! I've always hated you. Ever since your mom married my dad and forced us together, you've ruined my life. Ruined everything! But I'm going to finally fucking kill you for it... finally!"

Cameron lunged for Keegan, and Keegan screamed.

Keegan screamed, and all the Kin in the lodge fell to the floor in agony.

I was clutching my head, the pain searing in my skull. It felt like someone had set my mind on fire with the intensity of the sun; its heat leaking out of my temples. It was all I knew, all I was. It burnt away all conscious thoughts of Daniel Hale or of the Kin. My body, my identity, everything was scorched away with the noise.

I had no idea I had been dragged to the porch until the pain began to subside. I felt blood all over my face. Not a lot, but slight trickles from my ears, eyes, and nose. I had smeared it all over me. I still couldn't stand, but Keegan found the strength to hoist me up, and yanked me down the steps. Behind me, someone screamed out. One of the feral zealots.

Keegan said something but I couldn't understand her. I turned, hoping to make out her words and tumbled in the dirt.

Again, she yelled something, but all I made out was her swearing at me. This wasn't going well at all.

Climbing back to my feet, I was about to yell some words of encouragement at her, when pain bloomed in my shoulder. It spun me around to see Cole collapsing on the porch, with a gun in his hand. At least whatever was affecting me was still taking its toll on him. Staggering, I saw Keegan pointing to the truck, the keys in her hand. No words needed.

We bolted across the camp driveway, my senses returning to me quicker with every step. I opened the door and pushed her in, narrowly missing another bullet. Jumping behind the wheel, I gunned the engine and shoved the truck into reverse. Peeling out, I maneuvered the vehicle back down the road as Cole kept firing. The last thing I saw was him stop as Holly toppled out onto the porch. Spinning the truck around by some swings, I almost hit the trees on the roadside. We took off like bats out of hell from the property.

Keegan sat beside me sobbing.

"Thank you for saving me," I said quietly.

"Why was Cameron like that?"

"I don't..."

"What am I?"

I've seen terror before. I've killed hundreds, probably thousands of people. It gives me no real pleasure, but it sure as hell doesn't keep me up at night. By that standard, I always considered myself a sociopath. Charming, manipulative, devoid of basic empathy. But something about Keegan Pembroke tapped into a deeper part of me that was usually dormant. It made me curious, if not a bit uncomfortable. I wanted to know what she was, too.

Hell, maybe I'd be the one who'd end up eating her.

"I need to take care of this bullet wound," I said. "Maybe we can find some answers for you there."

"Where?"

"Home."

CHAPTER 18

KELSEY

What a clusterfuck.

The rest stop extraction had been messy. Turned out a carload of people had pulled in the parking lot and heard Mr. Ted Sheffield of Dayton, Ohio being abducted. Fortunately, they hadn't seen anything, and were too cowardly to stick around after calling the cops. We only knew they had been there because my dad saw them peeling out after he was sneaking back to get the tow truck.

Instead of the usual plan, we had to all climb back into the tow truck and stuff the Sheffields into the cab with us. It was uncomfortable and incredibly dangerous. If anyone would've glanced over during our drive back, they would have wondered why I was sitting on Jeff's lap, pressed up against the window. Not to mention there was a chance Ted could have come awake at any moment.

Leaving their car behind burnt that hunting site for us. The authorities would now link the couple's abduction back there. There was even a chance they would be able to trace back to the tow truck. Jeff was ready to kill both of them, and I had to calm him down.

"That would be pointless," I said as the truck drove up the hill towards home. "The entire hunt would've been for nothing then. We'd still have to go back out."

"Fuck these two assholes," he said pouting.

I rolled my eyes. It was a simple enough issue.

I had gone through Lily Sheffield's purse while we had been driving back, used her thumb on her phone, and gathered up information. Their names, home, careers, all that kind of stuff. It made it more engaging when it came time to taunt them. From what I had pieced together, they had been heading to the coast for their one-year wedding anniversary. How sweet. He was some type of mechanical engineer and she was a nurse. No kids yet. Not ever now. I wiped the phone down and tossed it before we were even two miles down the road.

Dad parked in front of the shack, and I leapt out. Jeff followed and began to heave Lily Sheffield out of the cab. She was all limbs and torso, that one, and he was having a difficult time with the dead, not-dead-yet weight. I should've offered to help, but I didn't. Dad heaved Ted over his shoulders and carried him inside. Both were tossed up against the wall, and the shackled pulled down on their chains, securely tightened around their wrists. Hoisted high until their feet barely touched the dirt, another set of cuffs were placed around their ankles once shoes and socks were removed. They were entirely suspended by iron, but only held taut enough to not swing. I enjoyed the sound the chains make as they squirm, it's a bunch of metallic squeals and dull rattles.

I examined my two new tributes and let some of the anxiety wash away. This was my church, and here I was priestess. Pith would watch over and reward me for this sacrifice.

"Thank you both, very much. I need some time with Mr. Sheffield here."

I could feel Jeff hesitating behind me until dad grabbed him by the shirt. I briefly wondered if Jeff was going to start becoming a problem but needed to dismiss that for another time. Now was a time for wonders and terrors. Lily would be out for another few hours, there was nothing I could do about that. That was the magic. Ted, however, could be woken.

After retrieving the smelling salts from a box on the table, I cracked it under his nose. He was roused with a start, gasping and choking. Sometimes they even vomited.

"Wha... where am I? Lily?"

"Give it a minute. What you experienced can be very disorienting."

"What the... who? Who the fuck are you?"

"I am Kelsey Radu of the Sect, and you are here to give yourself over to a greater event of divine purpose."

"What?"

"I'm going to torture you endlessly for days and feed off your fear to give birth to my god manifest in her human form. Doesn't that sound nice? It does for me, at least."

"You're fucking crazy," he said looking around. "Where's my... Lily! Lily, wake up!"

"Oh, she's going to sleep for another few hours. You're dealing with Magic, Ted. It's a game changer."

He scowled at me. "Let us go, you psycho bitch."

I went melodramatic, acted offended at his words. "Psycho bitch? Do you call Lily such horrible things? I bet you don't. I also bet you've never had your fingers set on fire and the flesh sloughed off with a dull knife."

Oh, the change his face made.

"What?"

"Here, let me show you."

I got one of those little propane torches that cooks use to make crème brûlée with and a box cutter. The smaller flame was easier to control with detail-work than the larger blowtorches plumbers used. Walking back over to him, he started blubbering. The realization was hitting him.

"You don't have to do this," he said. "We won't tell anyone!"

"Do you know how many times I've heard that, Ted. I want to do this, and I know you won't tell anyone."

We started his journey with the ring finger and pinky on his left hand. He screeched when that blue flamed roasted away the meat. They were two little hotdogs being grilled up. Smelled about the same, too. He thrashed around, but there wasn't much give in the shackles. They blackened up really nicely. Switching out for the box cutter, I began to carve off little shavings from the charred flesh. There really wasn't much left by the time I was done, the torch burnt almost down to the bone.

I had to hand it to Ted, he hadn't passed out. He had screamed, and sweated, and vomited, but he was still conscious. He may have pissed himself a tiny bit, as well. It was hard to tell. I deposited my toys back on the table and got a jar of salve. It had been enhanced with mystical properties. Slathering it on his ruined fingers, it wouldn't heal them, but it would prevent infection.

"Now let's see, Ted," I said, touching his forehead. "What do you fear?"

A swirling miasma of memories, nightmares, and phobias cascaded over me.

I chuckled as I peered down into his deepest psychic well. "So be it, Ted. Spiders it is."

CHAPTER 19

DANIEL

My car was still parked back at the bar, so I didn't expect there to be any vehicles parked outside Rosenthal's house. Instead, when I got us back, there was a black BMW sitting there. It was an older model probably from the mid-80's, but in pristine condition. That made me nervous. Rosenthal always parked his cars in the garage.

Keegan helped me out of the car and to the front doors. She had asked a few questions on the way there, and I had done my best to explain. I tried to assure her that Rosenthal wasn't going to eat her, that my mentor could be trusted. There were too many unanswered questions we needed help with from her.

We spilled into the foyer; Keegan was cradling me on the floor. I started to pull myself up when I realized there were three people standing above me. Three Kin. Rosenthal and two others. I immediately recognized the severe looking older white man, shaven completely bald of all hair. Koller, the man who had mentored Rosenthal. The ageless Asian woman was doubtlessly the legendary Mayumi, an actual Elder.

At this point I considered myself, and Keegan, right fucked.

"You're injured," stated Rosenthal. "Shot?"

"This is way worse than you lead me to believe," I said, getting to my feet.

"Interesting," murmured Mayumi, leaning in to observe Keegan.

Keegan clung to me and said nothing.

"This is Keegan Pembroke. She saved me. Her sister is a feral Kin now, along with three others. Holly is amassing her own little-pack."

"Not her sister," said Mayumi.

"Step-sister," whisper Keegan.

"Tell us everything," barked Koller, gaining him a stern look from Rosenthal who walked off to the kitchen.

I sighed and sat down on one of the chairs gripping my shoulder. "I followed the evidence Rosenthal collected and investigated Holly Freemont. Which led me to a bar where I met Keegan. She was looking for her sister, eh... stepsister Cameron. Keegan immediately knew I was a Wendigo. She read my mind. I figured we could pool resources. A telepath might come in handy."

"That was..." began Koller.

"That was smart," finished Mayumi. "Continue."

"We had made some plans and left the bar, when we were ambushed by one of Holly's boys with a gun. I figured it was the quickest way to actually find Holly. Plus, honestly, I didn't want Keegan to get hurt. I don't know why I felt that way, I just didn't."

There was no point holding anything back from them. Honesty was my only course now. I hoped the tactic wouldn't get us slaughtered right here.

"Of course, not," said Mayumi. "She's a cousin."

"What?" asked Keegan.

I had no idea what that meant and shrugged at the ancient Kin.

"She is Throng, she is of the Fey. By their standards, Keegan Pembroke here is an infant faerie."

I was floored. I had never met one of the Throng before. I could tell this information was even more a shock to Keegan.

"How... how is this possible?"

"I don't know young one, but power emanates off you too strongly for someone of your age. I've met many a Fey, and you have the capacity of those six times your lifespan. I fear whatever is affecting the Kin has burdened your kind as well."

I reached out and took her hand. "When did your powers kick in?"

"I've always kinda had them, but they became super active a few months ago."

"Damn," said Koller. "The timetable lines up."

Rosenthal returned with a plate of meat, and a knife. "Eat."

I dug in, knowing the steak came from a special stock of human flesh. It would heal me in a matter of hours. He even seasoned it with garlic butter, such a classy fellow.

"So, Holly has turned four more to Kin?" asked Rosenthal, his arms folded tightly across his chest.

"It's more than that. She honestly believes that Manaha is talking to her and wants her to go feral, to kill humans at will and make as many Kin as she can. She's a believer and she's teaching it to her pack."

Mayumi nodded. "We're running into this elsewhere. Whatever is speaking in The Mist; too many are susceptible to the Voice. They want to believe it is Manaha, they want to cast off centuries of safety. This is the first I've heard of a pack being formed like this, but it won't be the last."

I swallowed down the last bite, already feeling better. Except I knew my final bit of information wasn't going to be as appetizing.

"Holly doesn't believe in the Carrion Court. She thinks it's all bullshit Rosenthal used to keep her in line. And according to her, even if they do exist, she's ready to battle them. Any and all."

Kollar laughed. "Oh, the Vacant will love that."

"We only escaped because Keegan did some kind of psychic thing. We stole the truck and drove back here. That's everything."

"Alright," said Rosenthal. "Another steak for you, coffee for everyone else."

"I'll help," said Koller.

"Can I get you anything, dear?" Rosenthal asked Keegan.

"No thank you," she replied in a whisper.

The two men left the room and I scooted closer to her. "Hey, I know this is a lot to take in. Are you okay?"

"Daniel, do I... do I eat people now?"

"What? No! You... I don't know what you eat. Kin eat flesh. The Sallow, er... vampires consume blood. I'm not sure what Throng need to, um, survive."

"Belief," said Mayumi.

The Elder sat there, very proper in her chair with a slight smile. Her hair had a kiss of gray among the rest of a jet-black up-do. She had only a few wrinkles. Mayumi appeared to be anywhere between mid-forties and late sixties. She was ageless and beautiful. I knew she was almost four hundred. While she was Kin, she didn't identify as "Wendigo" but as an Aswang, a creature from the lore of her homeland. Many of us from around the globe did similarly throughout the Court. She was nowhere as terrifying as I expected her to be.

"Belief? How do I... what?" Keegan tried, fumbling over her words.

"The Throng are a psychic race, and belief is a rich conscious sensation. It doesn't matter what that the belief is in. I think that's what makes your presence here all the more fascinating."

"What do you mean?"

"We are currently about to wage war against a group of feral Kin who are plagued with a set of lunatic beliefs. I can't think of a better time to suddenly have a Throng on our side."

"But I don't know how to use my powers like that!"

"I wouldn't worry, little Fey. In times like this, even I might bother to believe in Manaha for a moment or two."

INTERLUDE 2

Detective Kenyon stepped out of the vehicle and surveyed the scene.

"What a shit show," Hayward muttered behind him.

Kenyon had to agree.

Over two dozen people ran around the rest stop and its property, approximately twenty-eight miles out of Ennis. Too many people. It had become a damn circus.

The State Highway had things badly roped off and were already trampling over everything like excited puppy dogs. It wasn't often they snagged a case like this. ECPD already knew it was linked to their cases, but the Staties had been willing to play nice. Captain Long had taken Kenyon aside and urged him to keep Hayward on a short leash. His partner could be the most charismatic guy on the force some days, hurling furniture through a window the next. Hayward had a particular distaste for the Highway Boys.

Along with their fellow officers, the Bureau of Crime Investigation and Interrogation had been called in. A state-run organization, they ran forensics for crime scenes in places too small to host their own facilities. Ennis, Ohio was lucky if it had a fingerprint kit lying around in storage from the 1980's.

"Eight-one?" a voice crackled over their radios.

"Send it, dispatch," Kenyon replied to his unit number.

"Chief needs an update," came the voice of dispatch.

"Jesus, we just got here," said Hayward.

"Copy," said Kenyon. "You'll have a SITREP as soon as we can."

"Standing by."

Hayward pinched the bridge of his nose and his partner shrugged. Kenyon watched his partner storm off toward the rest stop, and sighed. It was going to be a shitty morning.

Hayward had been a detective for a few more years than Kenyon, and he sometimes wondered if whatever John had seen in those years had hardened him. He used to be more jovial back in the day. Jarred Kenyon saw horrors day in and day out with his job, but he managed to keep it all compartmentalized. He didn't bring it home to Trish and the kids. They were his world and he didn't want them to see the uglier side of the reality.

Kenyon hated when he saw bad cops out there in the media. He took it personally. It made his job harder. Hayward teetered the line sometimes, but he was fueled by righteous anger as opposed to entitlement. Even Kenyon couldn't be too upset if Hayward bounced a convicted child molester's head off their car door when arresting him for the third time.

Inside the rest stop, it was as big a mess as they feared.

"Detectives Hayward and Kenyon, Ennis City Police Department," said Hayward, nodding at one of the Staties. "We're expected."

"Yeah, I was told this might tie into all that shit going down in your town. I'd tell you what we've got, but it might not add up to much."

"Something is better than nothing,"

The Statie pointed to the restrooms. "There were at least two of them, one for the wife, one for the husband. Probably more. The husband was beaten and the wife was either coerced or removed some other way. Maybe drugged, but there was no blood or signs of struggle in the women's restroom. They accessed the utility room and moved them out back then through the backdoor outside. We believe there was a waiting vehicle parked there."

Kenyon stepped through the doors and peered around at the trees. A BCI&I canopy was set up, two forensic techs taking samples of the dirt and measuring the tire trucks on the ground. The marks looked wide and fresh.

"We found some hair and some prints. Hundreds of them. Not going to help much," said the Statie.

"What makes you think this was more than one person?" asked Hayward. "Just curious."

"Moving two people in a short amount of time is hard," the State Trooper said. "Abducting them is harder. Plus, dealing with the locked doors and driving away? Had to be two. And this were a fit couple in their late twenties."

Kenyon and Hayward exchanged glances.

"What?" asked the Statie.

"It's a theory we've been floating back and forth," Hayward said. "Multiple abductors working together. We call 'em the "unnatural born killers". Our chief isn't a fan."

"Hey, I told you what we've got. You can add it up however you want."

Back in the car, Kenyon and Hayward sat there for a few minutes, both processing everything. It was obviously the same person or group who had been taking people in their town. The fact-patterns were too similar not to be the same. It was bizarre.

"You better radio back in," said Hayward.

"McVay is going to be pissed."

"Yep."

No one noticed the van parked across the street, and its occupants inside. Eyes on the crime scene, eyes on the detectives as they pulled out and headed back towards Ennis. The van pulled off the shoulder of the road and followed the Officers' Ford Explorer and headed south, back towards town.

Eyes that watched, eyes that waited.

CHAPTER 20

KELSEY

I didn't know where Jeff went that morning and I didn't care. I was in a good mood and I wasn't going to let anyone ruin it for me. It was a little chilly for September in Ohio at that point, day-time high of mid-seventies, but I was relishing in it. The breeze made me feel alive. I pranced out to the shack in nothing but my underwear and a thin, oversized tee shirt. Summer had been carrying these blue tooth speakers with her when we abducted her, and I "borrowed" them. I brought them along with my phone.

Today there would be music!

Ted was still in a magically-induced fever dream where spiders burrowed into his skin, laid eggs, and then burst out, only to repeat the process. He would be worthless for a few more hours until I brought him out of it. He looked disgusting hanging there unconscious, the shit, piss, and drool was collecting down his body. Well, I suppose that's what I had a hose for. Playtime with Ted would have to wait for later.

This morning was for Lily. I could hear her screams as I rounded the front of the shack. She began pleading as soon as I entered.

"Oh my god, please! Let me go... please!"

There was a glimmer of hope in her voice, as if she thought I might empathize with her, and just all of a sudden let them go.

"Lily, I already went over this with your husband. As you can see, he didn't take what I had to say very well." Pointing a solitary finger. "You're here, you're going to stay here, it's going to hurt while you're alive."

She began to weep, but wisely shut up.

On the table, I sat my stuff down and paired my phone up to the speaker. I was in the mood for something dark but soft. Lana Del Rey? Lorde? Broods? I picked Billie Eilish and let the bass come up along with the ethereal vocals. The shears looked inviting, so I lifted them off the table.

Swaying to the music, I made my way over into front of Lily. She was already rigid with fear and I loved it. Slowly, I began to slice fragments off of her shirt, working it apart until it was in tatters. She was slender, with pale skin. Her pert B- cups were held wantonly in a frilly blue bra. I'd get to that eventually, for now it was only eye-candy. Gently, the edges of the large scissors were running along the skin of her stomach and she tried not to quiver in terror. The scissor blades were probably cold against her bare-skin and she was still shivering from the night in the cold.

I leaned in and sucked that building fear right from her lips.

I'm not sure what it felt like to humans, but they always seemed emotionally-drained after the effect. Not terribly so, but enough that I knew to give them a few minutes before starting in again. That was fine, I had to make a deposit. Ruby was waiting.

Coming back, Lily was crying again. Dear god, did those big blue eyes shine bright when they had tears in them. I was definitely carving them out of her head before she died.

"Why?" Lily asked.

"I love that question," I replied. "Do you really want to know?"

She nodded. I knew this was going to lead down a road of suffering, but what the hell.

"I'm not actually human, I am Sect. You would call me a Witch. The Sect is part of the Carrion Court along with other, well... monsters. Each group of monsters has its own magic and its own god. That's all well and dandy, but there's a limited amount of magic to go around. I'm cheating the system and stealing magic from those other gods and monsters and giving it to my god. To do that, I have to kill a lot of people, including you."

Lily stared at me.

I stared right back.

"Aren't these other monsters gonna be pissed?" asked Lily.

I wasn't expecting that. No one had ever actually engaged me in dialogue before. I peered at her, taking in her slight curves and tear-soaked face. I had planned on retrieving a hammer but discarded that idea. Now I ran my finger along the top hem of her jeans.

"Yes, conceivably. Very pissed and very capable of destroying me. But that would mean they had figured out what was going on here before I even completed the task... And, I'm already two-thirds done, I'd say. By the time they deduce what's happening and manage to track me down, I'll have succeeded."

"I... I could be a Witch. I could help you."

I sighed. This, unfortunately, was the second time I'd heard this.

"No, Lily, you couldn't. You must be born one."

"You could teach me!"

She was only grasping at straws.

I ran my hand across her skin, feeling its smoothness. My head against her chest, I breathed in her scent. Pretty. I kissed the small valley between her breasts and held back tears as I went to the table. Despite all these people in my life, I still felt alone. My baby wouldn't be able to fix that. I hoped Pith would.

So much for my good mood.

I changed the music over to Beartooth and picked up a pair of needle-nosed pliers. Without a word, I marched over and began pinching pieces of skin as hard as I could underneath Lily's right tricep. She screamed and tried to pull away, but I held her in place with my free hand. Again, and again I pinched her with the pliers until bits of skin were gouged out and blood ran freely. A dozen times until that section of her arm was a mass of gore.

Licking the flowing wounds, I pulled a chuck of flesh out with my teeth. The wailing was glorious. I could feel my nipples rock hard under the thin shirt.

Fuck this girl for making me feel hope. All I needed was horror.

One hand holding her in place as I licked and tore away at her brutalized arm, blood pouring over my mouth and chin, my other hand slid down the front of my underwear. Her terror was my pleasure, and that's the way it should be. It was exquisite.

As I orgasmed, I clamped my fingers hard around her mouth and sucked all of that delicious fear out of her. It got placed inside Ruby and I left the shack, music still playing, no salve applied. I didn't care.

I didn't care.

CHAPTER 21

DANIEL

K oller returned carrying a tray of coffees and passed them out. He sat down, sipping his drink and fell into whispers with Mayumi. I'd met him once before but didn't care much for the old German. All I knew was that he had found Rosenthal in the trenches during World War I and shown my mentor the path of the Kin. I got the impression they hadn't spoken often during the last half of the century, but I didn't know if they had a falling out or if that was simply the way of our kind.

Rosenthal glided back into the room with another of his special steaks for me and a sandwich for Keegan. It smelled delicious and she looked up at him expectantly.

"A grilled cheese of smoked gouda and asiago with sun-dried tomatoes on sourdough bread and a thin pesto sauce. You need your sustenance, and I thought perhaps serving you anything with meat in it might be taken the wrong way."

Keegan smiled, tears welling. "Thank you, so much."

Rosenthal didn't know how to process her show of emotion, and awkwardly patted her on the head. I almost choked on my steak.

We both tore into our food, occasionally stealing glances from each other. At least I knew why I had these feelings for her now, but in a way, that didn't change anything. I felt connected to her, protective of her. I had found women physically appealing before, but this was different. I found myself powerfully drawn to her. Yes physically, but it was more than that. Those big brown eyes held so much emotion, more than I was ever capable of having. I wanted to touch her dark skin, not necessarily in a sexual way, and in no manner violently. I was having trouble with all of it and kept trying to push it out of my head.

"You know I can read your thought, remember?"

God damn it.

"Please don't fall in love with me," she whispered.

"I'm a sociopathic wendigo," I replied. "I'm not capable."

She frowned at me.

"You are really hot though. Sorry."

She snorted a little laugh. "How did this happen?"

"What do you know about your background?"

"I'm a mutt! African-American, Pakistani, English, Dutch, and French. No faerie in there."

"I don't know how it works with the Throng. It's not passed down through Kin bloodline, not the way you think. It's more... magical, I guess. Then again, I know it is a hereditary thing with the Sect."

"Who?"

"Witches."

"There's Witches, too?"

"Yes dear," interrupted Mayumi. "Wendigo, Witches, Vampires, Faeries, and Djinn. The five Tribes that make up the Carrion Courts. That's what we were discussing. If you are being affected, perhaps other faeries, other Throng, are as well. And if that's the case, one would think this could be affecting all in the Court."

Koller leaned back in his chair. "Unless one of the Tribes is behind it."

"To what end?" asked Rosenthal.

"Sow discord. Make us weak. Does it matter?" his mentor replied.

"It does matter," I said. "If we discovered Motive, that would lead us to which Court. Power is what the Sect want, chaos is the Vacant's game. The Sallow and the Throng both want order, just by different means. At least, this is all what I've been told, mind you."

Mayumi clapped and Koller rolled his eyes. Rosenthal actually looked pleased.

"And what do we want?" asked the Elder.

"To be left alone. Freedom, I guess. It's conceivable we did this to ourselves, but..."

"No," said Rosenthal. "There were always outliers in the community, but before this, we were relatively unified."

"So, we agree this isn't Manaha?" I asked.

"Also, affecting the Throng? No, I think not," said Mayumi.

"Then what has this kind of power?" I mumbled.

The room went quiet.

Neither us nor those dusty blood-suckers could pull off something like this. The Throng were a powerful race, but this seemed to go against everything they stood for. They had been the leading voice in assimilating with the humans back in the day, and still championed that stance. The Sect were organized but not necessarily powerful enough to achieve something like this, while the Vacant were unbelievably powerful but scattered and disjointed.

Keegan raised her hand. "May I ask a question?"

"Of course!" said Mayumi.

"If I understand this correctly, this... Manaha, he's your spirit animal or god or something? Of the Kin?"

"That's correct."

"Do the faeries, um... the Throng, have a god?"

"Yes, Larcre," said Mayumi. "But they don't worship her any more than we usually worship Manaha. She's more a symbol, like the Christian's have their cross."

"And the other tribes, they have gods?"

"Where are you going with this?" asked Koller.

"People going crazy, invisible voices, people forming cults," said Keegan. "I dunno, maybe this is about the gods or something. Not them really, but more conceptually. I wouldn't know or think about this faerie god if my powers went wonky, because I didn't know what I was. But, would a Throng who did know about their god? Would a Sect know?"

Rosenthal downed the last of his coffee and turned to Mayumi. "It's a decent theory."

"A possible 'why' but still not the 'who,' unfortunately," said Koller.

"Have you heard any voices?" I asked Keegan.

"Yeah, but it's all been like you and other regular people. Nothing creepy and god-like. I can hear a bunch right... oh, shit!"

"What?"

Mayumi stood up. "The Ferals have arrived."

CHAPTER 22

KELSEY

Smoking behind the trailer again. I found a pair of old gym shorts and slipped them on before sneaking back and lighting up. A plume of smoke burst from my mouth and I began to relax. There was no reason why Lily should've rattled me like that. I had to keep my eye on the prize and not waiver. Everything I desired would be achieved at the end, and all my dreams would be granted.

I was relatively sure what was going on out there. The Kin were going insane, the Sallow were becoming lethargic, the Throng were losing control, and the Vacant... well, who knows what was happening with those weird bastards. It was all because of the Fear. Because Pith was growing in power, his influence on fear would be cascading over the other Carrion deities and down upon the tribes. The more fear, the more strength Pith would have to manifest in the vessel. In Ruby.

By now, the other tribes were probably starting to figure out something was terribly wrong. There would be squabbling and finger-pointing, maybe even some oh-so important meetings would be scheduled amongst the elders. I wasn't worried. Enough of the Sect were aware of what I was up to, we passed word on what to say if any members of the Court came calling. The party-line was to reply that our access to magic was waxing and waning. All bullshit, of course, but they didn't need to know that. The Court would run itself in circles of political intrigue for weeks. Or so, I had been advised.

I don't know how much I trusted my so-called "advisors," but the plan was sound. A group of Elder Sect had visited us shortly after Ruby's death. Like, I'm talking only hours afterwards. We hadn't even finished building the funeral pyre for her.

Ruby had attempted to channel Pith as a means to jumpstart a certain curse. She was feuding with a local human girl and her sister for years, and something had happened, some line was crossed. But, I'm still not sure what the Elders were so interested in. Ruby was reaching out for deeper black magic, but she needed the energy to fuel it. It was too much, like trying to power a car with a nuclear plant. She had tortured five people, soaked in their fear, tapped the Carrion Fields, and she burnt-out. I heard her screaming from the house.

Just so you know: two weeks later, I poisoned both those bitches who drove my sister into that reckless shit.

Anyhow, my mom was still sobbing as my dad and I were gathering wood for the bonfire when a trio of Elder Sect showed up. Even through her lunacy and tears, my mom had the good sense to be scared. Their names, as I would come to find were Annette, Masozi, and Eloa. They appeared to be maybe in their fifties or sixties. I later learned that they were hundreds of years old; their lives had been extended by magic. They were dressed in contemporary fashion, although they all wore black hooded cloaks denoting their stations.

After introducing themselves, Eloa turned to my mom. "We felt the passing of our young sister. We grieve with you."

"Thank you," whispered my mom.

Eloa's tanned, wrinkled face pulled into a smile, her eyes falling on my grandma. "I've met you before, Judy Beaumont. You were a child then, when I told your grandmother what I tell you now – you have a wonderfully powerful and unique bloodline."

Grandma snorted. "Not powerful enough, I reckon."

Eloa chuckled, but Annette frowned. "No living being is powerful enough to channel a Carrion God."

"No living being," added Masozi.

And thus, began our little mission. Naturally, my mom was against it at first. She was against it all: Ruby's body being used, the risk I was taking, and the general threat to the family. Grandma and I talked her down, along with a strong urging from the Elders.

I guess all of this was foreseen by some prophecy. Ruby's body had been primed as a vessel when it touched the minor fraction of Pith's essence before it killed her. Only a blood relative of the vessel could feed it the needed fear to continue on. As it turned out, I was one of this generation's most adept Sect.

Hearing that was an ego boost. While Pith wasn't strictly bound to identifying with any particular gender, the prophecy spoke of two sisters. Finally, everything was supposed to take place in a desolate location. I had to laugh at that one, because Ennis, Ohio definitely fit the bill.

Eloa and Annette came back a few more times to check on our progress and to teach me how to proceed with the incantations. Annette never said much, and I could tell she had reservations about the whole scheme. Eloa was kind and informative, and I learned as much as I could from the old Brazilian. Mom hated her, but I caught her and my grandma giggling about something once on the porch. That warmed me to her even more.

The Elders gave me their blessings and our hunts began in earnest. One victim used to sustain the entire household for almost two months. After the ritual started, we were painting the shack in fresh blood. Maybe mom wasn't getting enough fear, I don't know, but she started getting worse around this time.

She had paranoia, delusions, screaming fits. She looked for every excuse to wail about her "poor dead Ruby". I pointed out one time that her and Ruby could barely stand to be in the same room with each other. I got a plate thrown at my head.

Ruby had been my best friend; she was everything I wanted to be. More outgoing, more courageous. A little shorter, but with actual curves. She even had better, thicker hair. Everyone said we looked the same in the face, but I never saw it. Maybe the same big brown eyes, I don't know. She was stronger, funnier... better. I was so unbelievably mad when she left me, and I miss her every day.

But wherever she was, I was going to make her proud. If I can be honest, I might've been doing all this for me, but I felt I was doing it in her name.

CHAPTER 23

DANIEL

Rosenthal leapt from his chair. "They must not have realized yet that the others are here or they wouldn't have been so brazen."

"This is our best opportunity," said Mayumi, untucking her shirt.

I grabbed Keegan's hand and pulled her to her feet, empty plate clattering to the floor. "Come with me!"

"Where are..."

Without answering, I dragged her across the hall and up the steps. Through the upstairs and into my room, I sat her down on the floor opposite the bed. From here, she had at least some coverage. Opening the closet, I tore through it until I found a lock box and yanked it open. Inside was a large revolver.

"Here," I said, shoving it into her hand. "It won't kill our kind, but it will slow us down. Don't open the door for anyone but me."

"Daniel!"

I kissed her on the forehead gently, and rushed back out of the room, locking it as I went.

"Don't go in The Mist!" she cried out behind me.

I didn't have a choice.

Jumping down the stairs, I ripped off my shirt. I could already hear the battle raging. The Mist came and I began to transform. My skin went to its death pallor, antlers sprouted, legs reshaping, tufts of hair grew, claws elongated, and my jaw redeveloped. I brought it on too fast and there was so much pain. Reaching the bottom of the stairs, I received a kick to the groin that sent me hurtling into a wall. I looked up to see a Kin standing over me.

His thoughts came to me through The Mist. "You're gonna learn, pretty boy."

Nolan.

He brought another foot down at my face, but I dodged it, swiping up at him with a claw. I hit him at the back of the calf. It was only enough to piss him off, but I was standing upright again. Nolan raised his hands to rake me with his claws and I dove into him, crashing him through the banister. I raised a claw, but then we were both startled by a howl in the kitchen. A piece of wood clocked me on the side of the head, and I tumbled off the stairs.

Staggering back, I began to hear the Voice.

The mumbling from all sides, with the roar underneath. Shadows and light growing sharper in my vision. My senses became more acute, some fragrances were assaulting me.

My Child, love the beast that you are.

My Child, give into all flesh, yours and theirs.

My Child, listen to Manaha.

It was too much, too intense. Not just the words, but the sensations. Overwhelming. All my senses in overdrive, taking in too much stimuli to properly process. It was agony.

I fumbled around clutching my head. I felt claws shred my back but didn't know how to react to that sensory input along with everything else happening. It was no better or worse than anything else I was experiencing. I wondered if I gave in to the voice if it would stop.

Through The Mist, I heard Nolan laugh. "Manaha has you. You should have accepted him sooner."

There was a stir in the air. I knew Nolan was preparing a killing blow. There was nothing I could do. All of my senses were dialed up full blast.

Then there was a new Voice.

THIS IS NOT MANAHA! THE VOICE HAS LIED TO YOU!

The Voice of Keegan Pembroke, strong and loud, broke through the psychic barriers holding me.

IT IS A TRICKSTER, SEEKING CHAOS AND DEATH, FEEDING YOU HOLLOW PROMISES! YOU'VE BEEN MANIPULATED FOR ANOTHER'S GAIN. LOOK INTO THE MIST AND SEE THE TRUTH!

I was kicked back into reality, pain blossomed throughout my shoulder. Across from me, Nolan was transforming back into his human form, trembling. He peered at me with watering eyes.

"I just wanted to be a savage, man," he said. "Hardcore."

There was no point in giving him a response. In one swift motion, I gutted him open from groin to throat with my claw. He didn't even try to hold his organs in, just letting them spill out as he collapsed on the carpet.

"Why?"

I turned to see Thomas standing there, back in human form.

"We... we know now! Why would you do that?"

With a slight nod to her, Mayumi slunk up behind him and rammed her whole arm through his head, obliterating it. Obliterating him.

The pack hadn't been sanctioned, their transformation into Kin was never approved by the Elders. Cured or not, they were never walking out of that house alive. There had to be order among chaos. Fortunately for us, it looked that having their beliefs stripped away had stripped them of their need to fight, as well.

I wanted to check on Keegan, but this wasn't over yet.

CHAPTER 24

KELSEY

I had work to do.

Ted was awake once more, gasping and moaning. I could hear the chains shaking as he shook them while I stood just outside and beyond their sight. Lily tried to console him, tried to calm him down, but she could barely control her own tears.

"Baby, it's okay, It's alright," she said. "I'm right here, we're going to be okay."

Such lies.

"The spiders," replied Ted, slurring the words. "Where... they were everywhere."

"No spiders, baby! No spiders, she gave you some kind of drug, made you see things."

Oh, I'd make them see terrifying things.

"No... no spiders. Okay. Where, what are..."

"Ted, you've got to stay with me, I need you!"

"Yeah, yeah, I'm sorry."

"We've got to get out of here," said Lily. "She's going to kill us."

Ted rustled in his shackles. "Where is she now?"

"I don't know. She, she took off about an hour ago."

"What the fuck happened to your arm?"

Lily didn't respond.

"What did that bitch do to your arm?" screamed Ted.

"I'm so scared, Ted."

That's what I wanted to hear.

I strolled into the shack holding a plastic grocery bag, beaming smiles at both of them. Ted looked like a bag of hammered shit and Lily instinctively pulled back from me. Honestly, I was proud that Mr. Sheffield could form full sentences. Their bond must be strong. I was going to enjoy exploiting that.

"What the fuck did you do to my wife?" bellowed Ted.

"I had a good time with her," I said. "What are you going to do about it, spider boy?"

He swore and thrashed in his chains but was impotent to respond in any meaningful way. One of my favorite things in the world to do is swipe away that illusionary power and privilege from white cis males. That moment when I see they finally realize that the little sexually ambiguous girl in front of them has all the authority in room. Seeing that is always the highlight of my day.

I paired up the speakers again and this time picked something a little more fun. A bouncy number by Panic! At the Disco hit the speakers, as I slipped on the brass knuckles, and bopped over to Ted. He was still cursing at me and wasn't paying attention.

I hear Brandon Urie puts on a great live show. But I put on an even better one. Ted was too busy yapping, he was probably convinced I was groovin' out to the music. I was getting closer to him. Close enough to bust him in the mouth with the brass knuckles.

The surprise shut him up and made me laugh. Still laughing, I went back over to the table and sat them down. Now I retrieved a sharpie, one of those plain black ones. Ted was blubbering through a few broken teeth, but now Lily started up.

"Please, we don't have much money, but we'll give you all of it. Anything you want."

"Don't care about money, Lily."

"You... you can take the rest of my clothes off."

I turned and scowled at her. "Oh, you're gorgeous, and I'll be taking your clothes off more than likely, but not for the reasons you think. I'm not some rapist fuck. Every last gasp of fear will be ripped, hammered, and burnt out of you before I dump your rotting meat sack in a ditch behind the garage."

"You're insane," she said with tears flowing. "You're not a witch. You're just a crazy girl."

"I was hoping you'd say something like that."

Over at Ted, I began to draw a complex glyph on side of his abdomen with the sharpie. One big circle with a smaller circle inside, a triangle on top pointing down, three lines on each side, an arc bisecting the bottom, and then a series of tiny symbols at the four corners. With a deep breath, I began an incantation.

"What are you doing?" asked Lily.

I ignored her, ignored the shack and everything. In my focus, all I knew was the magic, Pith and his will. Their energies flowed through me. Reality became malleable.

My fingertips touched the side of Ted's torso, skin to skin, then I passed through. He made a high-pitched sound, his brain unable to process the sensation. I slipped my hand into his body and gripped hold of his lowest rib. There was a liminal moment of silence, of transition and expectation. Then the snap came.

Ted howled in agony and my hand slid back out of his body, his skin was completely free of wounds or any blemishes. I turned to Lily and opened my fingers. There laid a four-inch section of Ted's rib, broken off and covered in blood.

"No," protested Lily, the word drawn out in terror. "No, it can't... you didn't actually do that. It was a trick!"

"You watched. You know," I said.

"No!" shrieked Lily, pulling way from her in horror, the realization enveloping her. She had watched. She now knew I wasn't lying.

In three paces, I was over to Lily Sheffield, my hand clamping her mouth open and draining out that fear. There was so much, and I indulged a bit this time. My strength was growing as Pith grew closer.

Both the Sheffields hung in their restraints, broken. Still enjoying my music, I continued tormenting both of them in petty little ways. Both my grandma and mom would be making a trek down to shack later that night to feed on their fears, so I had to make sure the Sheffields were prepared. Tessa hadn't come into her powers yet, but it would only be a matter of time.

I had been going back and forth between fiddling with Ted's broken teeth and snapping Lily's fingers with a lobster cracker. I was in a good mood again. At some point Jeff must have come by and seen me toying with Lily. He knew what had to be done to acquire the fear, but he had also pieced together that I preferred a certain type of person to play with.

A person that wasn't like him.

CHAPTER 25

DANIEL

Mayumi and I rushed into Rosenthal's spacious kitchen. I didn't know if everyone had been accounted for, and worried that someone might have made it upstairs. Even with the power of the Voice lifted, not every member of the pack might be as manageable as Thomas and Nolan had been.

My concern ended up being all for nothing. Cole and Cameron were on their knees, fully transformed back into humans. Cole looked confused, and Cameron simply sobbed beside him. Koller was half changed, blood was pouring out from a wound in his neck. He looked ready to fall at any second.

Rosenthal was still in full form, with Holly backed up against the sink. Although she had reverted back to human form, her face was one of defiance. The claws pressed to her throat had changed nothing for her.

Without deliberating, I took off Cole's head in a swipe before he could question anything.

"Wait!" screamed Cameron, holding up her arms.

Mayumi reared back, claws ready.

Cameron's eyes found mine. "Tell Keegan I'm sor..."

Cameron's head rolled onto the kitchen tile.

I transformed back into my human form and looked to Holly. The hate radiated from her. Whatever spell had been lifted from the others wasn't the same one here.

"Go on, kill me too," she spat with rage.

"They weren't Kin who were approved by the Elders," said Mayumi, as she reverted back. "Any rogue Kin are exterminated. I assume Rosenthal taught you this."

"Oh, he told me a lot," she said. "Act this way, don't do that. Behave and hide like a scared kitten. Ten different ways to say 'control.' You're all pathetic."

I got it then. She had these beliefs before the Voice.

"You would rather have anarchy?" asked Mayumi.

"Yes!" roared Holly. "To feed and fuck like the superior beings we are! Paths of blood behind us, a throne of bones and crowns of entrails. We deserve nothing less!"

Rosenthal had transformed back enough to speak. "My god, you should have never been approved for Kinship."

Head held high, Holly said, "I'm the only one worthy in this room."

Mayumi glanced to me and then to Koller. "Can you make it into The Mist?"

His eyes gleamed. "Yes."

I knew what was coming.

Even my empty, black heart was stunned.

"Holly Fremont, as an Elder Kin, I find you guilty of feral activities and unlawfully creating others of our kind," said Mayumi. "Present for this verdict are Kin Erich Koller, Gerald Rosenthal, and Daniel Hale. Your sentence is death."

Holly snorted. "Better dead than your slave."

It took her a moment to realize we were all changing form. Perhaps she thought death was going to come swift like with her companions. They hadn't been approved Kin. She had, and therefore her crime was considered more severe.

"No, not like this," she said, trying to bolt out of the kitchen.

Mayumi's hand caught her and hurled her to the ground. No claws were used, no blow that would injure. No, Holly hit the tile and was momentarily stunned, but quickly understood her predicament. Those few seconds were all we needed.

Koller, Rosenthal, Mayumi, and I pounced on her and began devouring her alive. She screamed as we ate her, tearing off body parts and digging into organs. I think she tried to find The Mist but didn't have the strength. Jaws snapped through bones, tongues lapped up blood, mouths gulped down meat. More and more of her disappeared.

Feeding on another Kin was forbidden unless under edict from an Elder for a death sentence. I could see why. The flesh was sweeter, richer, and I knew would keep me at maximum for months. Outside of any truly grievous injury, I would be at peak condition for quite a while.

We all finished and sat back, our human forms returning. None of us looked at each other. This didn't really feel like a victory.

"Go check on your young Throng," said Mayumi. "We need to thank her."

CHAPTER 26

KELSEY

By the time I finished with Ted and Lily last night, everyone had already eaten dinner and scattered to the winds. I helped both grandma and mom down to the shack and let them feed privately on their own, then walked them back up to the house. Dad assisted me at that point. Both ladies were in much better moods after supping on that fear, but it didn't make moving them any easier. Mom could only take so many steps before wheezing and pushing a wheelchair through grass was an effort.

We left both of them in the living room, its screen playing an inane sitcom. Dad said Tessa was in her room and Jeff was out in the garage. There were leftovers in the fridge. He kissed me on the head and went out to work on one of the cars.

It was just rigatoni and meatballs tonight, but I was starving. I pulled the crockpot that was stuffed into the fridge on the counter and heaped a gigantic portion onto a paper plate. After I put the crockpot back, I kicked the door shut and threw the floppy plate into the microwave. I considered going up and seeing what my little sister was doing, but she was probably up there on her cell phone, texting friends. I had no one to text. Tessa was more adjusted to human society than I ever had been. She actually "fit-in" at school. I decided not to bother her.

Eating my plate of food with the blare from the television coming in from the next room, it hit me how tired I was. I was tired more often anymore. It was likely the baby. I kept thinking about how I was going to have to schedule an appointment with the clinic, then remembered the entire point of what I was doing. Clinics wouldn't be open for much longer...

I finished up, dropped my plate in the garbage, and wandered down to my trailer. Slipping out of the clothes I had on, chances are I was asleep before my head even hit the pillow. I didn't even hear Jeff come in.

I certainly heard him banging around the next morning.

Fumbling around for my phone, the screen told me it was shortly after six am. Still dark outside. What day was it? I couldn't remember, and I honestly couldn't remember if Jeff had gotten another job yet. I rolled over and pulled the covers over my head to drown out the noise he was making.

Even under the blanket, the smell of coffee came to me. Warm and dark, it beckoned. Grumbling, I threw back the covers and tossed around the clothes on the floor until I found a frayed zip-up hoodie.

In the narrow kitchen, I found Jeff pouring a mug. He was still wearing the clothes he had yesterday, which didn't mean much for him, but I got the impression he had been up all night. I didn't know if he had been working with my dad or off playing on his own, but the smile he gave me seemed a little off.

"Hey baby," he said. "You didn't need to get dressed."

"There more coffee?" I asked.

He poured me a mug and topped it off with the hazelnut creamer that I liked. With a smile and a thank you, I reached for the mug. It was a cheap but delicious French roast, made perfect with the sweet tones from the creamer. I had been drinking it every morning since I was twelve.

Between sips, I noticed Jeff eyeing my legs. The hoodie barely came down low enough to cover my naked ass. It wasn't necessarily my ass he was thinking about.

"It's too early, Jeff," I said, cutting off his line of thinking before it got too far.

"Jesus Christ, Kelsey," he said, throwing his half-filled mug in the sink. "It's always too early. Or too late. What's with you? We used to fuck like rabbits."

I stared him down over the rim of my mug. "Don't you fucking raise your voice at me."

"Is it the baby? It is some hormone thing?"

I blew on my coffee and took another sip. "Yeah, it's a hormone thing."

Jeff rubbed his face and stared at the ceiling. "Do you still love me?"

"Yes."

And I did. Just not in the way he wanted me to. I knew that. And my love for him wasn't as strong as my love for the baby growing inside me. That baby came first. And with that baby, came my mission for Pith.

"Did you snag that couple so you could play with the wife?" asked Jeff.

This was a predicament. Lie or tell the truth? Perhaps a bit of both.

"Partly, yes," I said. "She was beautiful, and happy, and in love. I wanted to exploit that, ruin that. Multiples are always better than solo victims, you know that."

He threw his hands in the air. "Kelsey, do you want to fuck her?"

Damn.

"Not anymore, no."

It was all the anger washed out of him, leaving him defeated.

"You can fuck her if you want," I said. "Would that make you feel better?"

"No! You've told me that crap before, and I've always told you no. I only want you! I never really understood why you were so damn keen on throwing me victims, but now I get it. It's so you wouldn't feel bad for cheating on me."

"I've never..." I started to say, then realized what was about to come out of my mouth.

"What Kelsey, what?"

"It's for the fear, Jeff! If there has to be a sexual element then, so be it. Do I enjoy it sometimes? Fuck, yes! I am Sect, not human! You knew what you were getting into when you signed up for this."

Disgust, confusion, anger, resignation. Myriad emotions passed through him as I reamed him out. Finally, he went stoic as he picked up his stuff off the table and headed towards the door.

"I picked up a three-day labor gig down the river in Alleywood. I'll be home late tonight. I love you."

And he was gone.

The couch caught me when I collapsed onto it, tears coming. I did love Jeff, but he was making it difficult. He couldn't get in my way. Nothing could. He had come into my life when I needed him there, and given me the gift growing in my belly, but things had changed. He couldn't be a distraction.

Jeff would either have to get with the program or he'd have to go.

CHAPTER 27

DANIEL

"**K**eegan!"

I took the stairs two at a time, banging on the door as I screamed Keegan's name.

"Keegan, it's me! It's Daniel. Can you open the door?"

The door was still locked. I pounded on the door again.

"Keegan, don't shoot, it's Daniel! Can you hear me? Can you unlock the door?"

From inside, I heard a faint moan. A voice calling my name.

I brought The Mist enough to transform my arm, and in one swipe, tore the door from its hinges.

Inside, I scrambled around to the side of the far side of the bed where I had left her and stopped stunned.

Her dark, flawless skin had turned a deep, glowing pink, and her long, black curls were now a vibrant, almost metallic purple. Each breath she took, on the exhale, pulsed the glow brighter. Keegan stared at her hands in horror, the clothing she wore was doing very little to conceal her inner light.

"What... what's happened to me?"

"I think this is the magical form of the Fey. The Throng, I mean. Your form," I babbled.

I pushed the bed out of the way and grabbed a pair of shorts lying nearby on one of my open suitcases. I crawled down next to her and wrapped my arms around her shoulders. Keegan quietly cried against me.

"Am I going to be like this forever?"

"I don't know."

The tears came harder.

"We won thanks to you," I said. "and I would've died if you hadn't helped."

"I could hear their thoughts, their madness. Some other voices, but not, like... the Voice. I dunno. I had to do something."

"Well, it worked."

We sat there for a minute before I hugged her and said, "Cameron, uh..."

"I know. I heard her apology at the end, too."

"Good. I'm sorry."

"It wasn't your fault, it was Holly Fremont, and whatever got inside her head."

"Holly's not a problem anymore."

Keegan shuddered. "Yeah, I know that, too."

"Oh, by the way, in case you haven't noticed," I said letting go of her. "You're not glowing anymore."

Sure enough, she had almost completely returned to normal, except her black hair still had a slight purplish sheen to it. It was actually quite striking, and only looked like she had paid a salon to give it a remarkable dye job. Keegan examined herself in the mirror and found it acceptable.

"You helped calm me down, Daniel," she said, playing with her hair. "I guess that's why I changed back?"

"Aspects of your Throng form will always become physically apparent now when you access your powers," said Mayumi from doorway. "How much you transform will depend on how much power you access."

"But I can always sorta read minds," said Keegan.

Mayumi smiled. "You will always sorta have purple hair."

I laughed out loud at that one.

"Please, get cleaned up and dressed. We have to discuss something with the two of you."

I exchanged glances with Keegan and shrugged. Instead of worrying her with wild speculation, I showed her where Holly had stored some extra clothes while I took a quick shower. Afterwards, I changed into bootcut jeans, a gray tee shirt and slip-on black shoes. This outfit was easy to discard for a quick move into my other self.

I did my best not to ogle Keegan when she walked out. She wore a white tank top, red and black checkered flannel, jean shorts, and black boots. The boots were a little big on her, but she had found some heavy socks that made them fit better. On anyone else, it wouldn't have been the sexiest outfit, but for some reason I couldn't stop beaming at her. Was she blushing? Hell, she was reading my mind again.

Downstairs, all the bodies were gone, although the place was still wrecked. Rosenthal was hastily attempting to clean off some of the furniture so we all would have some place to sit that wasn't covered in blood or broken glass. Honestly, I think I would've killed Holly simply for being mean to that poor man, he was a saint.

"Gerald, that's fine," said Mayumi. "Everyone, please."

We took what seats we could and waited for the Elder to speak.

"Keegan Pembroke, we cannot thank you enough for your intervention here tonight. It is very likely your actions alone saved at least one of us."

"She definitely saved me," I said.

Mayumi nodded. "I will see to it the Throng Elders hear of your commendable actions and you receive proper accolades and training from your people."

"Thank you," replied Keegan in a meek voice.

"We still don't know what this Voice was or its true intentions. However, the fact a single young Throng was able to dispel it confirms the Elders' theory that it is indeed not our Manaha. Koller and I merely stopped here on our way towards another destination, but now we feel we must return to the Carrion Courts and make our findings known."

"Other destination?" I asked.

"Southeast Ohio. If you look at a map of feral incidents, a pattern emerges. Something is happening in Southeast Ohio."

I felt like I already knew where this was going.

"Daniel Hale, you've proven yourself more than capable in both battle and investigative work. I'd like you to travel down to this region and see what you can discover. Keegan Pembroke, I can ask nothing of you, but only say whatever is there is quite probably the source of whatever infected your step-sister's mind. Each uncovered clue brings us one step closer to ending this plague."

I began to stand. "That's not fair to..."

"I'll do it," said Keegan,

"Are you sure?" I asked.

"I'm the brains, you're the muscle," she replied with a grin.

"I don't know about this," I said, sitting back down.

"She'll learn quick," grumbled Koller.

"One last thing," said Mayumi. "Daniel Hale, under my authority, with Erich Koller and Gerald Rosenthal as witnesses, I hereby deputize you as a Longtooth."

My eyes went wide. "What the fuck does that mean?"

"You are now one of the elite guards of the Kin," said Rosenthal with a grimace. "At your discretion you may kill any member of our kind with impunity."

CHAPTER 28

KELSEY

It had been a productive day torturing Ted and Lily.

I successfully pushed Jeff out of my mind and concentrated on my goals. Both of the Sheffields had managed to shit themselves during the night, so I used the shears to cut off the remaining bits from their clothes and took the hose to them. I did my best not to gawk and Lily's glistening body. I couldn't get distracted in that way.

Instead I decided to get rid of some of that pretty pale skin. I let the flames build up in the fire pit outside while I staple gunned Ted's penis to his belly, removed the staples with pliers, and did it again. His curses were laughable without any front teeth. Meanwhile, I was heating up some low temperature, homemade pitch.

The stuff is easy to make and vicious. Crushed charcoal, sawdust, beeswax, and a few other minor ingredients. Heat, mix, and brush on vulnerable skin. It was an abrasive, bubbling concoction that dried quickly, and set as hard as plastic. I had to be careful ladling the substance from the caldron into the bucket. A few drops had splattered on me before, so I had firsthand experience on how painful it was to scrape off afterwards. You'd be lucky if you had some water to throw onto the wound to remove some of the heat, but my victims had to suffer through the burns until I was ready.

Back in the shack, there were no words, no explanation - the pitch merely began getting applied. Lily's shrieks were ear-piercing. Her skin blistered immediately, torn open and burnt from the rough, smoldering goo. Patches on her legs and arms were coated haphazardly because the stuff cooled down pretty quickly. A nice big X across her torso. She passed out before I could do anymore, so I took to the bucket back outside and carefully dumped the rest back into the caldron. When it dried, the blisters would make her skin would slough away like a roasted pepper.

She wasn't so attractive anymore.

I spent the rest of the day toying with Ted, making him talk to me. He liked Star Trek and Lindsey Stirling, and preferred hazelnut creamer in his coffee, too. Lily played guitar and was devoted to their dog, Moxie. They were decent happy people until I found them. But they were just people, after all.

I was something else, something more. Ted and Lily Sheffield would've never been friends with me. I would have been just another white trash girl to them if I hadn't shown them the truth. The world needs to see the truth.

It was late into the evening when I was cutting Ted's nipple off. Lily had come around again and was moaning in pain. I still hadn't seen Jeff yet, and wasn't worrying about it. An amusing idea about reattaching Ted's nipple somewhere naughty had popped into my head. Lifting his leg, I began to summon up magic, when there was some kind of stutter in the energies.

The magic kicked-back, and I was knocked across the room.

I wasn't hurt, more simply stunned. Nothing like that had ever happened. I tossed the nipple and shot to the back of the shack were Ruby hung high in ceremonial preparation. Lily let out another moan as I passed her.

"Dashoon!" I yelled, tilting my head, knocking out both of them.

Kneeling down, I drew a symbol in the dirt and began a litany, seeking out ripples in the magic. It was a clairvoyant eye, they're not always reliable, but it's the best I could do on short notice. I brought my head down in supplication, my forehead to the dirt. I closed my eyes and let my mind see.

Pale flesh, claws, and fangs. Blood that flowed and flesh that tore. Kind against kind, Kin against Kin. Pulled from the dream, cured of the fever. Five less walk high.

I snapped back, trying to make sense of what I had seen. There had been a battle, perhaps? Some Kin had killed their own kind, five dead. Five that had been under the influence of Pith and our magic.

There was a chance that things were moving faster than I anticipated. Could the Court actually have figured out what was going on? Even with as much power as I had amassed in such a short time, there were still things I couldn't do yet. But others could.

I raced to the house, hoping my grandmother was still awake. Judy Beaumont didn't sleep much anymore, her arthritis kept her up. Sure enough, as I burst in the front door, she was awake and watching television.

"What's got you all riled up?"

"I need you to roll the bones," I said.

She leaned back in her wheelchair and squinted at me. "What's happened?"

I explained everything, leaving out no detail. Grandma growled and spit, then rolled herself towards a cabinet. Fiddling with it, she gestured for me to grab a candle.

"I had a feeling the Elders and their timing was for shit," she said. "Let's see what we're dealing with.

She rolled the bag from the cabinet over to the dining room table. One complicated hand movement shut off the television, and a word brought the candle to life. I sat beside her as she reverently opened the bag and brought out the finger bones of her grandmother, each one etched with Sect runes. Pushing back the tablecloth, a circle was deeply scored into the wood.

The bones cupped in two hands, she shook them over the circle, chanting, "Ellba, Kammi, Rifter, Vlaum!"

She released them. Of the twelve bones, five stayed in the circle and the rest bounced out. My grandma examined the runes on those five bones.

"Five Kin are dead," she said.

"I believe so, yes."

She scooped them up and did it again. This time ten stayed inside. She scowled at the runes.

"There's Throng involvement in this."

"God damn it."

"The rest is... shrouded. You're gonna need more clarity than this old woman can provide."

I knew what she was saying. It was time to go directly to the source.

It was time to speak with Pith again.

CHAPTER 29

DANIEL

God damn it.

I had heard about the Longtooth, of course. They were basically the police force of our kind, a handful of them rumored to report directly to the Elders. I assumed they had extensive training or were Elders themselves, not some random shmucks who got decrees laid on their heads. Don't get me wrong, I understood. There was a good chance we were going to come across more Kin out there who had succumbed to whatever the Voice was, and Keegan may not always be able to save me. Technically it was a crime if I killed another of my people without Mayumi "deputizing" me, but I didn't want that burden. I didn't want anyone of this.

Except maybe Keegan. I tried not to watch her pack and concentrated on my own tasks. I grabbed a small satchel and headed into my bathroom to get away from her for a few minutes. I didn't want to, but I needed to.

Throwing my shaving kit and mouthwash into the leather case, I glanced up in the mirror. I had no idea what I was doing. I wished somebody else saw that I was clueless.

I had been a loner for decades. Few friends, even fewer love interests. The only thing I was good at was thievery and other assorted criminal enterprises. Suddenly, I run into this Throng-chick and everything is chucked sideways. I was feeling things I never had before, and it confused the hell out of me. Confused, curious, and pissed off.

I wanted to protect her. I wanted to run my fingers up and down her skin. I wanted to kill in her name. I wanted to cry in her lap.

Everything left in the bathroom got crammed in the satchel and I head back out. Keegan was done packing and she was straightening up the room. The last of my things went in a suitcase.

"Is that everything?" she asked.

"I think so."

Downstairs Mayumi went over the map and the directions one more time, Koller was grumbling in the corner. Rosenthal had packed me a cooler of special steaks just in case, and I thanked him. I could tell he was uneasy about the whole thing, so I tried not to let my own nervousness show. In an uncharacteristic move that I blame on Keegan's influence, I gave him a hug. For a moment he was startled, then embraced me back.

Outside sat a black 2017 Mercedes S-Class that was all gassed up for us. Classy, reliable, but not so posh it would attract attention. Keegan dumped her stuff into the trunk and slid into the passenger seat while Mayumi gave some last-minute instructions.

"Be prepared for anything," she said. "Other Kin, other Tribes, new players."

"Gotcha."

"Call Rosenthal once a day with your progress."

"Understood."

"Leave a detailed message, it will be for more than his ears."

"No problem."

"Daniel," she said, taking my face in her hand.

I turned to look at her. The emotion there was unreadable.

"Be careful."

"We will, thank you."

My own grandma had been a drunken harpy. I'd let Mayumi adopt me.

Opal, Indiana swept past us tree by tree, and I was glad it was disappearing. My return home wasn't what I had anticipated it being. It was worse in some ways, and better in others. I remember thinking that I'd give it another twenty years again.

"So, tell me, how is it you're able to go off on a dangerous mission for an undetermined amount of time?" I asked

Keegan sighed. "I finished my bachelor's degree in psychology last semester. You can't do much with a BSA in psych, but I wanted to wait a little bit before going into my masters'. Just burnt out with school, you know? I've been weighing my options, technically living at my parents, but pretty much crashing at my friend Wendy's house."

"Okay, won't Wendy get worried?"

"Wendy's kind of a flake," Keegan said with a shrug. "She's lucky to know what day it is. I'm surprised she got through her undergrad. But hey, C's get you degrees! She'll assume I'm at my parents, and my parents will assume I'm with her."

"No job?"

Keegan groaned. "Three semesters of quantitative methods and a lab internship made me unfortunately good at statistics. I had a position doing data entry at a company, but it was sucking my soul away. I quit last month."

If I hadn't seen the fear on her and been saved by her twice, I would've been suspicious. But no, she was too green and too terrified. Still, it worried me.

"Would it make you feel better if I called Wendy and told her I was going to Ohio?"

Damn mind reading.

"A text would do. In case something happened."

Keegan pulled out her phone, fingers flying across the screen.

"There," she said, holding it up.

Sure enough, a text to a "Wendy" said she had met a cute guy and was taking an impromptu road trip to Ohio.

I knew I was blushing at some of her word choices.

"We cool?" she asked.

"Yeah, sorry. I'm Just all paranoid now. This Longtooth thing is kinda heavy."

"I know. You'll be fine."

It occurred to me that she probably knew I was freaking out about what Mayumi had done. In a way, that made it better. I had been clutching the steering wheel way too tight and tried to relax.

"What do you want to listen to?" I asked.

"What do you listen to? Elvis? The Big Bopper?"

"Fuck, I'm only in my forties!"

She found this terribly amusing. "What's that then? Hair metal?"

Swearing with a smile, I connected the car's audio to my phone. I tossed the phone over to her, showing a playlist with Machinegun Kelly, Odd Future, Mac Miller, and others. A beat started playing announcing a song by hip-hop collective Brockhampton.

"You listen to this?"

"It's one of the major tenets of the Kin. Adapt or die. Never cling onto the past, always evolve with the times."

Keegan raised an eyebrow. "Did you put on hip-hop because I'm black?"

"What? No! I... I love this, I wouldn't, not that... why..."

Keegan laughed. "You're so easy to fuck with."

She cranked up the volume and the Mercedes roared out of Opal into the unknown darkness.

INTERLUDE 3

The Delight Diner was one of those old trolley cars that had been converted into a café back in the 1950's when trains were all the rage. The place still stood today, an utter shithole, but the food was glorious. It served your standard fare of burgers, fries, and milkshakes, nothing special, but all of it was delicious. The burgers dripped with grease and molten cheese, topped with crisp lettuce and tomatoes bought that day from the produce stand right down the street. Giant baskets of fries were a natural cut, cooked to a crispy golden brown, bottles of ketchup and vinegar at every table. Known for their milkshakes, you could barely get any through a straw they were so thick. Sure, they had salads and grilled chicken, but no one went to the Delight for healthy selections.

Today John Hayward wanted to cheat on his diet. A bacon double cheeseburger and a chocolate shake. It had been that kind of day. Kenyon wasn't about to argue. His own wife had him on a diet as well, one he grumbled about daily.

The detectives stepped inside the diner and surveyed the clientele. As always, the response they received was mixed. Waves, eye rolls, scowls, general indifference. All that from only nine people. Fortunately, the table at the rear of the diner was open, so they could sit with their backs to wall. It sucked that they had to keep their awareness up all the time, but that came with the uniform.

They had started to take their seats when a middle-aged waitress came over to them. Her hair was a mess, and she looked exhausted, but managed to pull out a smile for them.

"Boys, what can I get for you?"

Hayward rattled off his order, added an iced tea, and looked to Kenyon.

"I'll get the same," said his partner. "But throw on a side of fries, too."

"Be right back," she said, gathering up the unread menus.

After she was back behind the counter, Hayward squinted out into the glare beyond the windows. "We've got to figure something out."

"Forensics is going to take forever," said Kenyon. "We need to connect some dots."

"The Chief is going to call in the FBI if we don't have a break soon. While I'm not opposed to getting help, I'm not handing the case over."

"Agreed," replied Kenyon, shutting up as their drinks arrived.

They both took sips after their drinks arrived and ruminated in their own thoughts for a bit. Hayward was trying to deduce why anyone would kill that many people, in such a variety of backgrounds. Serial killers all had their preferred types, blondes, brunettes, fat white men. This felt too random to be a serial killer. Kenyon concerned himself with some of the local assholes they knew who might fit a profile for psychopathy.

Their food came and both detectives dug in. After a few mouthfuls, Hayward took a gulp of milkshake. Perfect comfort food.

"So," began Hayward between bites of his burger. "You with me on serial killer?"

"Maybe. Or a cult. Hell, could be a cult that does the killings."

"Hmmm... that could explain the multiple perp theory. I'd believe that around here. We've met a lot of weirdos."

Kenyon swiped a fry through some ketchup. "Christ, it could be aliens for all we know."

"Yeah, let's tell Captain Long in the next report it's aliens."

"Well, I know you originally didn't like the idea of multiples, but it's looking more likely the longer we examine it. Sure, they prefer young women, but they would snag anybody. That rules out sex trafficking to me."

"Damn, and a lone killer would have a type," said Hayward.

Kenyon shrugged and took a bite.

"Let's go with your cult theory. Are they kidnapping them, brainwashing them, killing them? What do you think is happening after they disappear?"

Kenyon let out a breath and shook his head. "Hell man, I don't know."

"I might... huh."

"What?"

Hayward stirred his straw around in his milkshake. "Jen had this friend in college that studied religion and sociology. I don't remember her name, but she teaches at Bowling Green University now. Specializes in cults and weird shit. She might be willing to talk to us."

"Hey, she could tell us if we're on the right track at least!"

"I'll have her reach out."

"In the meantime?"

Hayward looked out the window again. The sun had disappeared behind some cloud and it had gotten gloomy outside. He took another bite of his burger, determined to finish their meal, despite having an appetite as fleeting as the daylight.

"If asked, we have a working theory and we're consulting an expert. Hopefully, that'll buy us some time. But we shouldn't offer-up too many details."

"Agreed."

CHAPTER 30

KELSEY

Jeff had stormed off again that morning, pissed at what I was about to do. He said it was because of the ritual that I had to partake in to commune with Pith, the hallucinogenic herbs I had to take, but I think it was more the communion itself. Sure, he cared about the baby's wellbeing, but his possessiveness was getting to be overbearing.

Whatever, he had taken one of the cars and left.

I didn't even bother toying with Ted and Lily. A quick Dashoon, and they were both out. I did check the wounds under the pitch on Lily, but everything seemed sealed nicely. What remained of Ted's penis was seeping a foul-smelling cloudy ichor. Excellent.

Back in front of Ruby, I set up two red candles to my left, two to my right. A large black candle was lit on top of an ancient quilt with Sect symbols embroidered into it. It had been given to me by the Elders specifically for this purpose. Colors long ago faded, yellow stitching now gray, purple embroidery now brown, all that black was now just dirty and faded. I sat on one end, the other half of the rectangle out before me. The black candle's flame illuminated the symbols there, the mantra I would need to speak, its words in a tongue never before heard by humans.

I had been given a half dozen doses of the herbs, told to use only if necessary. They contained a number of natural ingredients, some known to cause visions like bits of psilocybin, salvia, and mescaline, but along with other elements. Magical items that would be instantly fatal to anyone not of Sect blood, things like belladonna and hemlock. Altogether, this would propel me into what was referred to as the Carrion Cradle, sometimes known as the Carrion Fields.

Where the gods lived.

I was told to prepare the herbs either in tea or smoke them. Obviously, I smoked them. A big, fat spliff. With each exhale, I said a line on the blanket out loud, smoke billowing out of my mouth. The effects began to hit immediately. More hits, more lines from the blanket. I swear Ruby began to shift there from her perch on the wall. I laid down and curled up on the blanket, still smoking and reciting the litany from memory. Thick pungent smoke filled the back of the shack. The light grew dimmer with each puff.

Kelsey.

I stood up. I was naked and the shack was gone. Everything was gone except the smoke. It went on for eternity in all directions but for the blanket I stood on. Bluish-gray clouds swirled and floated in a deeper black darkness, and I was barely illuminated by something outside rationality.

Kelsey.

I spun towards his voice, her voice, the voice of Pith. I fell to my knees upon the blanket in devotion. I had been here twice before, but still felt such overwhelming reverence.

Rise, my anointed one. Speak.

How does one speak to a god?

"I... I have discovered the Kin are in league with Throng. A Throng. It has cast off the spell placed upon some of the beasts. I don't... I simply seek your guidance, Holy One."

Fear not the Vacant and the Sallow, for they continue to lurk as the Throng are in turmoil, and the Kin were never a concern. It is but this pairing that you speak of that may darken our great undertaking, for they indeed draw closer to you even now. It is you they seek, even if they do not recognize it yet. Be prepared.

"Thank you, You Greatness," I said. "I will make preparations."

Thank you, my child, for your endeavors. Come, let me love you.

Have you ever been fucked by a god? It is... transcendental.

The smoke began to billow faster and take shape. Warm and soft, it caressed my body. The temperature rose and as aspects of the smoke grew more solid. I was lifted off the blanket and hovered in the air, a hundred almost-hands running their fingers tips across my skin. A woman's breast slid across my face and I sucked on a nipple. Smoke-like hands pulled my arms high above my head and my legs were spread apart.

Tongues licked away at me, three, four, five of them. I began to buck my hips against the mouths between my legs, aching for more. Teeth lightly grazed my nipples, teasing me. A finger reached up behind me and gently rubbed. Ecstasy washed over me, but Pith wasn't done yet.

Legs spread wider, I began to be filled. Right to the point of almost too big, just perfect. Even more tongues came, lapping away, tasting me as I was taken. My nipples were sucked in rhythm to the thrusts as I took a nipple in my mouth and massaged my breasts with my hands. My mind was filled with images of skin and sex, the sounds of moans and screams. I felt a thousand Sect before me here, here before Pith, and we all came in unison.

And then I was back.

I lay on the blanket, sweaty and exhausted, the candles almost all burnt out. It was nearly time for dinner, almost eight hours had passed. Ted and Lily were awake and weeping.

I could see why the Elder only gave me so much of the Herb. I would go to Pith everyday if I could. Not that he would want me to commune with him so often. Still, I was reinvigorated and had some vital information.

Walking out of the shack, I glanced back over at the Sheffields and considered what to do with them next. They were starting to get boring. I'd think of something. For now, I needed food. I hoped dinner could go by in a normal fashion.

CHAPTER 31

DANIEL

Turring, Ohio.

We had driven the rest of the night and into the morning. It was time to stop and get some rest, find some food. I could have made it across the state without any issues, but I could tell Keegan needed more than a leather seat and a granola bar. I didn't know if we were exactly on a set timeframe, but Armageddon could wait a few hours.

I found one of those rinky-dink motels off the highway, a few franchise fast food joints across the street. Pulling in, there were at least a half dozen cars already in the lot plus a couple big rigs. I parked and Keegan climbed out, eyebrow raised.

"What?" I asked.

"Nothing."

Inside the office, a diminutive man with a bad combover was fussing about the desk. He looked up expectantly at us. "Can I help you?"

"I need, uh... two, one..."

"One room with two beds?" Keegan chimed in.

"That's all rooms, little lady!" the manager offered cheerfully.

"Great, we'll take one."

"Well, I can put you down for 104, but none of the rooms will be ready until 11:30."

"What time is it now?" I asked, realizing I left my phone in the car.

"10:36," said Keegan.

"Oh, that works out. We'll grab some food across the street. Here, how much is it?"

I paid the man what ended up being a reasonable price and the two of us sprinted across traffic to the restaurants. We had burgers, burgers, chicken, burgers, and tacos. We were about to give in to the shining lights of a burger place, when I spied a small diner that had breakfast all day. I gave a nod to Keegan, who side-eyed me.

I laughed. "What? I like breakfast food."

"This isn't exactly an urban metropolis."

"So?"

"Okay."

We strolled over and I opened the door. The first thing that hit me was the scent of bacon and maple syrup. Next were several hard stares. A few truckers in the corner, an old couple in a booth, a solitary man at the counter, even the waitress. Hostility radiated from everyone, outside of the single sad look from the cook peering at us from behind his station. At first, I didn't understand it. Them Keegan whispered in my ear.

"They don't want me here. Don't want us here together."

"Oh, fuck that," I said, stomping in.

I sat right next to the man at the counter and gave him a huge grin. He returned it with face full of disgust, threw some bills down on the counter, and left. There was some grumbling throughout the diner, and the waitress stood there, glowering at us.

"Patricia!" came a shout from the cook. "Wait on the customers."

She said nothing, simply raised her pen to her notepad and tilted her head.

"Gee Patricia, I don't know," I said, picking up a menu. "I was thinking pancakes, but now I'm more inclined for eggs. What do you think? Do I dare splurge and get both?"

"Daniel," came Keegan's voice from beside me.

I had already seen them get up out of the corner of my eye. Honestly, I was hoping they would. The three truckers shambled over in their stained jackets and red hats.

"Time for you to leave, boy," said the first one.

"And take your lil' darkie wh..."

My fist came around and caught him in the throat before he could finish the word. I went into The Mist just enough to give me heightened senses, to make me a tornado of hands, elbows, knees, and feet. I battered the three down in under a minute, leaving them in a bloody, broken pile.

Everyone in the place was terrified except for Keegan, who looked to the ceiling and sighed.

"Any other comments?" I asked.

No one said anything, no one moved.

"Yeah, I'm still hungry," Keegan replied.

"Let's go."

We ended up at one of those damn burger joints.

Nothing was said about it until we were in our room. I was glad when Keegan had climbed into bed. She had stripped down to a pair of shorts and a tank top in the bathroom, and I was desperately trying not to notice she was no longer wearing a bra. Of course, she knew that I had noticed, and I think she purposefully wandered around the room a little longer just to torment me. Regardless, she was under the covers and the lights were off, the blackout curtains were surprisingly good for a low-end motel. I could hear her rustling around.

"You okay?" I asked.

"Did you know that was going to happen today?"

"With those racist hicks? No. Well, I figured something might go down once we went inside, but at that point it was a matter of principle."

"Why?"

"I wasn't going to let those bumblefucks make you feel like that."

She didn't say anything, so I continued.

"I wanted to kill them," I said. "But that would've been a bit public. And I would've had to kill everyone in there. Plus, I knew you wouldn't have supported that."

"No, I would not have liked that."

"It's like... I'm trying here. Okay? To be better."

There was a pause, then she asked, "Why?"

God damn it.

Because for the first time in my miserable life I feel something real for another living thing. Because you make me want to be the person you want me to be. Because I finally am seeing a future beyond tomorrow and all of those days feature you in them. Because I think it's possible that I'm capable of love and I'm currently falling in love with you.

I didn't say any of that, of course. No, I was too much of a coward. Maybe I thought it as I lay there in that motel bed, my mind racing. Who knows? Hell, maybe she caught snippets of my true feelings. Looking back now, I hope so. I hope with all my heart. But at the time, it was too much.

So, I said: "Because."

I rolled over and set the alarm on my phone for 7pm.

I'd deal with tomorrow when tomorrow came.

CHAPTER 32

KELSEY

Another family dinner. From the start, I knew this one wasn't going to go well.

Mom was wailing about Ruby, how her precious first-born daughter wasn't here with us. How she was taken from us. The table wasn't even set yet, and mom was rewriting history. Angela Radu knew full well that Ruby had misused magic to her own end, that her death was her own fault, but she never wanted to hear that. They may have screamed and fought in life, but her daughter somehow became a sainted memory in passing.

It didn't help that my grandma was egging her on. Sometimes I don't think my grandma liked her own daughter very much. It was hard to tell. She sat there in her wheelchair, poking and prodding the delusions along, cackling as they got more exaggerated. Every now and again, someone would tell her to stop, but she'd brush us off and continue. Grandma had always been nothing but sweet to me and my sisters, but there was some tension between her and my that mom I could never quite figure out. For a time, I thought it might be my dad since he wasn't Sect, but she honestly liked him the best.

Tessa and my dad had finished up with cooking most of dinner. Tessa had cut all the vegetables for a giant bowl of salad - lettuce, onions, tomatoes, green peppers, cucumbers, and olives. Using a step stool, she was tall enough to mix everything on the countertop. I was that short at her age, too, until I shot up in a growth spurt.

My dad had come home and found my mom in her state, unable to care for herself today. He'd thrown two pans of frozen fries in the oven to bake while slicing up and frying a few pieces of thin steak that had been marinating since yesterday. He had just pulled the fries out when Jeff wandered in and was directed to set the table. That's when I arrived.

I felt bad that my dad had to cook. He worked over sixty hours a week to keep the lights on and keep us feed. Cash could be supplemented from what we found on people from the hunts, but it was never all that much. I would happily get a job, but my options were limited as a seventeen-year-old high school dropout, plus I had the mission imparted on me by the Elders. Tessa was too young, grandma too old, and mom was too crazy.

Then there was Jeff. I had no idea where he had been all day. I didn't really care, but I hoped he'd been out making money in some fashion. He bounced from job to job, usually getting fired, always with an excuse. It was never his fault. He finished setting the table and helped Tessa carry the bowl over, making some crack about the tomatoes that got her giggling. Times like that was a knife to the gut. He was better with Tessa than I was. I didn't know what to say to her after Ruby had died.

Everybody sat down, the bowl was getting passed around so heaping piles of salad could go on everyone's plate. Then a layer of golden crispy fries, followed by shredded cheese, then sliced steak. There was Italian, Thousand Island, and Honey Mustard dressings, but I went with the old standby, and drizzled Ranch all over mine. I snagged one of the pitchers of sweet tea and filled my glass to the brim before taking a swig.

Mom was still ranting even as we dug in. It wasn't terribly uncommon, and we'd all learned how to tune her out. Her shrieking and crying was merely background noise at this point. I wasn't paying attention until she hurled a fork at my head.

"What the fuck!" I yelled.

"I won't lose any more of my babies!" she screeched.

"You won't, calm down!"

Her fists banged down on the table "No more magic in the shack! No more!"

"You don't have a say in this," I said, my voice low.

"My house, my law!"

That had been one of her favorite sayings when I had been growing up. I hated it then, and I hated it even more now. Fortunately, it was not her house, and my eyes slid over to my grandma.

"Kelsey will continue her work," said Judy Beaumont. "You will not interfere."

My mom rose from the table on unsteady legs, grabbing a handful of food from her plate and stuffed it into her mouth with her hands.

"Betrayal!" she attempted to scream through the food before waddling off into the living room.

We all sat there in silence for a minute.

"Should I take her food to her?" asked Tessa.

"I'll take it to her later, dear," said my dad.

We kept eating, the scene was over, then Jeff had to ruin it.

"Would it be so bad if you quit?" he asked.

"Quit what?" I replied slowly, knowing full well what he meant.

"The shack. All the magic stuff."

I put my fork down, folded by hands carefully in front of me, and locked my gaze on him. "Let me make this perfectly clear. My mother is insane and you are human. Telling me to quit magic would be like telling you to quit breathing. The magic comes first, the magic will always come first. I told you this years ago, and you agreed that it wasn't a problem. Is it a problem now?"

Eyes wide, mouth tight, his foot shaking under the table. Oh yes, it was indeed a problem. But he didn't say that. "No problem, just asking."

I went to back to eating and realized my dad had been gripping a steak knife through that little conversation. He knew as well as I did that the "Jeff problem" was coming to a head. It was just a matter of how it played out and when.

CHAPTER 33

DANIEL

Shortly after we woke up, Keegan said, "What's the plan now, boss?"

I made an excuse to go to the car, hoping I was out of range of her telepathy, so I could have a quick existential crisis. Boss? I knew it was just a figure of speech, but it freaked me out. People were depending on me. Sure, I'd had a handful of crooks look to me before when it came to jack a house or pull off some other heist, but this was different. This mattered.

I needed a reason. I had suddenly bolted out to the car in nothing but my jeans, so I popped the trunk and rooted around. Ever-cautious, Rosenthal had packed a map of Ohio along with everything else. I snagged it and went back inside. Keegan was giving me a funny look, but I pretended to ignore it.

"Look," I said, unfolding the map. "Most of the activity is further southeast in Morrison County. But we've had some reports about an hour from here, in Garthland. Two 'animal attacks' and a bunch of mauled livestock. It's on the way."

Keegan peered at the map. "That's gotta be probably two and half hours away from Morrison County. Do you think it's related?"

I sat back on the bed and ran a hand across my clippered head. "I don't know."

"Fair enough, let's get moving."

We finished getting dressed and packed up, grabbed some food from across the street. Keegan marveled at my ability to drive and eat tacos at the same time. It's a skill. We zipped down some state routes deeper into Ohio.

I had some dark electronica by Aes Dana playing as the sun went down and it started to rain. I found it atmospheric. Keegan thought it was creepy. She started scrolling through my playlists until she found Rihanna. I was okay with her, too.

While we drove, Keegan fed me information about Garthland off the internet. It's official city site and Wikipedia did not have much to say since not a whole hell of a lot was going on in the small village. Garthland was adjacent to a decently sized state park, however. That piqued my interest. Kin had been using state parks as playgrounds for decades, sometimes to kill, but often simply to go into The Mist.

I had a feeling I knew what may have happened here.

It was about nine at night when we drove into Garthland, and the town was already shut down. No cars, no movement. I could see light on as we drove down the quaint main street, but not a single person. You could see the place was already in decline, the shop fronts with grimy windows and the sidewalks crumbling. Houses were desperately in need of a paint job and the roads were pockmarked with potholes. Their census likely topped off at five thousand, that number dropping every year as the elderly died and the youth fled. For now, they all clung to the shelter of their homes, every one of them instinctively knowing that a predator was out among them.

The GPS looped us the wrong way, and we ended up driving out towards a farm. I realized immediately we had made a wrong turn and went to turn around. Backing up into a driveway by a barn, I had put the car back into drive when a light blinded me from the front.

"What 'choo doin' out here?" came a voice.

"We're lost," I said, rolling down the window. "From Indiana. We're just backing up, and we'll be on our way. Sorry to bother you."

"Indiana?"

A gruff looking farmer in flannel stepped over and lowered his flashlight. He frowned and leaned over to squint at the license plate. The rain didn't seem to bother him.

"Wherever you kids are goin', you get there quick. You best stay out of Garthland, sumthin' bad here. Be safe now."

"Thank you, sir!" Keegan called out as I pulled out from the driveway.

The farmer gave a brisk nod and disappeared back into the rain.

"Well," I said, half a mile down the road. "I'm inclined to believe something is going on here."

"Yeah."

We found the right road and turned into Garthland Memorial State Park, although we never did figure out exactly what it was memorializing. The roads were narrow, but well-maintained. Tall trees loomed in from both sides, their branches creating a canopy that shielded the car from some of the rain. The darkness here grew thick, cut by the illumination of our car's headlights. The scent of nature seeped inside the car, and I rolled down the window to breathe it in.

"What are you doing?" Keegan asked.

"Don't you love that smell?

"I guess. You can probably smell it better."

I snorted. "Kin, not werewolf."

"Shut up."

"I'm serious, though. Maybe it's because I..."

"Wait, no, shut up!"

"Huh?"

Keegan's eyes went wide. "There's someone else out here with us. I can hear his thoughts."

Running out from the roadside, a figure slammed into Keegan's side of the car. Her startled scream echoed inside for a moment as I hit the brakes and we swerved on the wet pavement. Throwing the Mercedes into park, I leapt out, at the ready.

The assailant was not what I expected.

A white male, he could have been anywhere between forty and seventy, his graying hair was falling out and his body looked emaciated and hungry. Bloody and filthy, he was wearing nothing but rags that barely concealed his skeletal frame. Most of his teeth had fallen out and cataracts clouded his eyes. He swayed while attempting to stand still, either in exhaustion or madness.

"Kin," he moaned, in a straining breath. "You are Kin."

"Yes," I said, taking a step towards him.

Keegan stepped out of the car, and he almost fell as he wailed. "Throng!"

"How did... yes, I am. How can we help you?"

I shot Keegan a look but focused back on the situation before me.

"Kill me!" he pleaded. "Kill me!"

CHAPTER 34

KELSEY

There wasn't much left of Ted at this point.

Despite my half-hearted attempts to keep him going, he was wheezing and seeping, barely coherent, and leaning into the last hours of his death. He'd lasted longer than most, given the abuse I'd hurled his way. Oh well.

I had painted some of Lily's open wounds with honey so flies would be attracted. Nobody liked flies. Unfortunately, this whole scenario seemed to have sent her over the edge. Broke her. She stared off into the distance, mumbling something I couldn't quite make out, as drool ran from the corner of her mouth.

I tried jabbing her with a small penknife a few times, but nothing. No response. Completely catatonic.

Damn.

It was still early and I assumed everyone had taken off for their daily responsibilities. Mine was supposed to be dealing with these two in the shack. Now it seemed they were worthless. Had I gone too hard? No, they had lasted as long as anybody else. I was simply getting anxious, looking forward for this all to be at an end.

Back in front of Ted, I started poking him with the penknife. "Hey, I think your pretty little wife is irrevocably damaged. You might need to trade her in for a new model."

One eye barely opened. Two words slipped from his mouth. They sounded like "fuck you."

There was no fear there, only hate and resignation. I'd been here before. It was a shame.

I considered different ways to kill him. Disemboweling, hot pokers, beheading. Most of those were used to terrify the people still living, but that would be a wasted effort in this case. The more I glanced back and forth between the Sheffields, the more disappointed I was.

One more disappointment in a long, ongoing list.

"Kakoom," I said, throwing out my hand with a swift rotation of the wrist.

Ted's neck snapped and he died unceremoniously.

I shouldn't have wasted my energy on magic like that, but I was frustrated. Taking a few steps over to one of the tables, I leaned against it and took a few deep breaths. I wouldn't have been able to do that spell two months ago. Rubbing my belly, it occurred to me that my skill had advanced a great deal in such a short amount of time. Part of it was all the training and power of Pith coursing through me, but part of it was the willpower I had found.

This little girl growing inside me wasn't going to be born into the same life I had been. I would tear down the whole damn world to ensure it. We both deserved better.

Ted was dead, and Lily was a space cadet. I didn't really know what to do. I'd wait until I had help to drag any bodies out of the shack. Since I had cigarettes stashed all of the place, I started searching until I found a half empty pack with a lighter stuffed inside.

Standing before Lily, I lit up and examined her. It was too bad. I could have enjoyed playing with her for a while longer. I honestly didn't know what to do with her. I wasn't going to waste more magic and thought about slitting her throat and being done with it. I had broken Ted's neck because it was a bloodless death, there was less to clean up afterwards. Planning out all of this was becoming a pain.

"Ah, Lily," I said, leaning forward and kissing her on the lips.

"I see you don't need any help."

Turning around, I found Jeff behind me, scowling.

Of course.

CHAPTER 35

DANIEL

"**D**ie! Wanna die!"

I stumbled back as the Kin flailed around wailing. He seemed like he was in pain, and utterly out of his mind. Not counting Holly and her crew, I'd only come across one other feral in my time, and it was savage—more beast than man. I didn't know what I was seeing here tonight.

"What's your name? Please?" tried Keegan. "Let us help you!"

"Name! I had a name!" shrieked the Kin.

He continued to fumble about, reaching out to both of us in agony, then pulling back suddenly as though he was fearful we'd treat him poorly. He kept babbling about being human, but only snippets of it sounded like actual words.

"... was a man, now dirt... tooth and claw, all red... voice demands..."

The Voice. The false Manaha Spirit.

"It's not real," I said, trying to comfort the man. "You have to get yourself under control."

He looked up at me, tears falling freely. "I know."

And then he began to transform.

Even as The Mist swirled around him, he took a swipe at me with his claws. I yelled for Keegan to get back in the car, our position too exposed. She slid around the front of the car as I started calling up The Mist to me. Before much of it could be summoned though, she released a psychic blast similar to the one she used at Rosenthal's house.

THE VOICE IS A LIE! IT IS NOT YOUR MANAHA SPIRIT, IT DOES NOT GUIDE YOU. BREAK FREE AND BE YOURSELF ONCE MORE. BE KIN.

The man falls back, human form once again. Sobbing, he curled up in a fetal position. Holly's zealots hadn't been affected like this either. I had no idea what was going on.

Keegan gently knelt down beside him, and he flinched as she drew near. Even worse than before, this Kin radiated fear and confusion. I began to wonder what he was like before the Voice had got ahold of him.

"You're okay now," said Keegan. "You're safe."

"Safe," he said, repeating the word and drawing it out like he had never heard it uttered before.

"What's your name?" she asked.

He scrunched up his face. "I had a name."

"Yes, what was your name?"

He stared at her.

"Okay, do you live around here?"

He looked around. "I don't know where we are?"

Keegan sighed. "What do you know?"

"I am hungry."

Uh-oh.

"You smell pretty."

God damn it.

"I'm a Throng," said Keegan.

"What's that?"

"You just... how can you not remember?"

Keegan hadn't been paying attention to me. I saw what was coming. I had been slowly drawing in The Mist. Before either of them noticed, I called up my claws, reached over, and sliced off the man's head.

The blood sprayed onto Keegan and she fell back screaming.

"Why? Why!"

"He was already damaged before the Voice got to him. The only reason he was aware of who we were was because the Voice told him. His behavior, his lack of knowledge – this was an unsanctioned Kin. No matter what, he was unbelievably dangerous."

"You didn't know that!" screamed Keegan, jumping to her feet and wiping blood from her face. "It was a guess!"

"I know enough about my people to make a very educated guess. You think I necessarily wanted to kill that guy? He was suffering, in the throes of madness even after being cured of the Voice's influence. I'm not the dude who does mercy killings, I'm not some valiant hero! I just rob shit, Keegan! This is way above my pay grade. But I knew that Kin had to go. That much, I'm sure of."

We glared at each other in silence for almost a full minute before she pulled off her flannel and used it to wipe away the rest of the blood. I looked away, not wanting to ogle her in such a tense moment. I went to the trunk to get a special set of supplies.

"You know, it's a good thing I'm psychic," she said. "I know you're not bullshitting me."

I didn't say anything. Instead I retrieved a small bag of powder and a road flare. Back at the body of the Kin, I began to spread the powder on him after I had set his head on his torso. I gestured for Keegan to place her flannel over his legs.

"What are you doing?"

"It's some stuff the Sect cooked up about three-hundred years ago. It Interacts with any organic compound and is highly combustible, but stable in transport. All members of the Carrion Court burn their dead so, humans never get ahold of us."

I struck up the road flare and dropped it onto the Kin. He went up instantly and was gone in a under a minute. All that was left was a scorch mark and some charred bits of clothing.

"Don't close the trunk, I'm getting another of Holly's fashionable flannels," said Keegan.

"You still pissed?"

She looked over her shoulder at me and pursed her lips. "I'm still something... I don't have the right word for it at the moment."

I glanced back at the scorch mark and nodded my head. "Fair enough."

CHAPTER 36

KELSEY

J eff stomped out of the shack swearing. Usually I would have
let him go, allowed him to blow off steam, and dealt with him
later. For some reason, I wasn't willing to drop it that day. I
followed him outside, cigarette still in my hand.

He was standing in the yard with his hands on his hips,
grumbling at the sky. Still dressed in a gym shorts and a ratty tee
shirt, it didn't look like he had any intention of going to a job
today. Spinning at my approach, he threw his hands up in the
air.

"What's your fucking problem?" I asked.

"My problem?" he replied. "Well first off, you're still
smoking, that's cute."

I took a puff, my face unchanged. "Yep."

"I thought..."

"You don't get to think about it, Jeff. I'm the mother, the
baby is in me."

That didn't sit well.

"Damn it, Kelsey! I'm the father of that baby, and you need
to respect that! Respect me!"

There was that word. Respect. I hated that word. Some
people believed that respect was automatically granted due to
circumstances, and that was utter nonsense. Should you respect
an elder without question, if that particular elder is an abusive
drunk who's gambled away all the family's savings? Should you
respect a partner who's cheated and brought home a sexually
transmitted disease? Should you respect a government that
cares more about corporate greed than it does the people it's
supposed to represent? No, that's insane. No, that's childlike
thinking.

Respect needs to be earned and given back in kind. It needs
to be gained through leadership, honesty, and strength of

character. It sounded like psycho-babble bullshit, but even I understood that.

I respected very few people. Jeff wasn't one of them.

"Why aren't you at work?" I asked.

"Don't change the subject."

"I want to focus on this subject. Why aren't you at work?"

"I'm looking for something closer to home, not that it matters."

I frowned. "Why doesn't it matter?"

"Because I should be here helping you!" he yelled.

"No, you really shouldn't."

Jeff sneered. "Or watching over you."

Dead stop. "What did you say?"

"You heard me. You're out of control. I think you're just using this ritual shit to live out your lesbo fantasies. Hell, even your mom wants you to stop."

"You need to stop talking right now," I whispered.

"No, you're going to listen to me for once! I'm sick of being pushed off to the side for your stupid magic, and I sure as hell won't be running in second place to a bunch of kidnapped whores. Things are gonna change around here."

Maybe it was earlier than I had thought, maybe my dad hadn't left for work yet. I don't know, it doesn't matter. I guess he heard the commotion and came out. One look at us in the yard and he knew.

He peered at me, locked eyes, and I sadly nodded my head "yes."

"Mike, stay out of this," said Jeff. "This is between me and..."

Before he could finish his sentence, my dad was behind him and slitting his throat.

He was caught before he fell, still gurgling out and clutching at the gushing wound. I went to him, pulled his hands away and stared into his eyes, telling him I loved him as the light died. No tears came, I'd save those for later. I didn't feed off his fear. Not Jeff.

My dad took his arms and I took his legs. We hauled him around behind the shack to where the other bodies had been taken. Speed was an issue, before Tessa saw. I knew it would upset her, and I considered not telling her.

"Tessa," my dad said, as if reading my mind.

"I know. I might say he got a job on the barges down river."

He grunted. "It'll work for a little while, but you'll have to tell her something else eventually."

"I know."

There was a six-by-six concrete slab behind the shack. While my dad stripped Jeff down, I raced back inside it and got a vial of Solskoldning Powder, powerful stuff made by a Danish Sect over three hundred years ago to get rid of Tribe bodies. You sprinkle it over any organic matter and, well, it burns right up.

Shortly, all that was left of Jeff was the pile of clothes we had tossed off to the side. My dad had his arm around me, and I still thought maybe those tears would come later, but now I wasn't as sure. Instead part of me just felt free.

"What happened?" asked my dad.

"He couldn't handle it," I replied.

"He was only human."

"You are, and you're awesome."

He chuckled. "I was raised by Sect my entire life. This way is all I know."

"That's true."

"Kelsey, you're going to be okay."

"I guess. Jeff was a mistake. He gave me this baby, and I'll always love him for that, but he wasn't the right one. I don't think... I don't know. It's the idea of him that I'll miss the most. I'm a terrible person for saying it, but it's true,"

My dad sighed. "Hon, you're young and Ennis is a shit town. You won't be here forever. You won't be lonely forever. Someday you will meet that right person, whoever he – or she – might be. Promise."

My eyes went huge, gaping at my dad, but he simply smiled at me and hugged me tighter. I guess it was a pretty well-known secret. I hugged him back before gathering up Jeff's clothes.

"Thank you, dad. I love you. I couldn't have... you know."

"I know. I'm always here for you."

CHAPTER 37

DANIEL

I put on some music by Apashe. Trap beats and classical samples laced in with rap lyrics. The noise was very high energy and good for keeping you awake while driving. I could also blare it since Keegan didn't seem inclined to talk to me.

She wasn't used to this life, I got that. I remember thinking that while I was glad she was next to me; she probably shouldn't have come along. It wasn't that I didn't think she could take care of herself, hell, she had already proven that. It was more complex than that.

Keegan was at her essence, a good person. She was honest, kind, and trusting. She may be Throng, but she wasn't emotionally built to handle the upcoming horrors. It's not that she wasn't strong, she just wasn't hardened. And I didn't want to see her hardened. I didn't want to see her become like me.

I tried not to think of all this too clearly while I was driving. Instead I let trees zip by under the cloudy night sky as I took the highway, few cars out in the wee hour. I had found a sort of comfort in the darkness ever since becoming Kin. My life was often nocturnal, like the night was another set of clothes I wore. I had never really talked to anyone about it, so I didn't know if it was a Kin thing, or if I was just weird.

I must have been musing about that, because Keegan looked over at me and said, "You're weird, but not for that."

"Huh?"

"A lot of people find solace in the night. Fewer people, less noise, things are more hidden or whatever. Plus, night has that connotation of being evil and sinful, and some people are drawn to that."

"You think I'm sinful?"

Keegan rubbed her temples. "No, I think... I picked up bits of your thoughts earlier. I think you're the definition of morally gray. You pick and choose your ethics like someone would food at a buffet, tossing bits aside when you no longer find them appetizing. It's better than some people, but it's definitely not me."

I had already turned the music down to listen to her, but now I turned it off. Her words struck home, and I couldn't argue with her analysis. Did I even want to? I realized the only reason I did was to make myself look better in her eyes.

"Here's the thing," she said. "When we came upon that poor guy back in the park, what was your first instinct? What was your gut reaction on how to deal with him?"

"To kill him. Not only was he under control of the voice, but..."

"It doesn't matter. The first thing you thought was to kill him. My first thought was to save him."

I shook my head. "You didn't understand the full story. The ramification of what we were dealing with. You still don't."

"Maybe, but that's not my point. That situation has passed now. If we open the next door, are you going to walk in and immediately assume you have to kill someone? Because I'm going to set out to save someone. Killing should be a last resort."

See? A good person.

Nothing was said for a few minutes. I didn't know how to respond. While part of me agreed with her in theory, in practice I felt she was being incredibly naïve. In the world of the Carrion Court, in the world she was now a part of, you had to assume everything out there wanted to tear off pieces of you and devour it while you watched sobbing.

"Daniel?"

"Yeah?"

"What are the rest of the Throng like?"

I glance over at her. She was frowning and picking at her fingernails.

"You're the first one I've ever met," I said.

"You've had to have heard stories over the years."

"Yeah so, from what I've heard, the Throng are kind of control freaks. Real big into the bureaucracy of the Carrion Court. They're tight with the Sallow, too. Eh, the Vampires. They were the loudest voices for integration with the humans, so I guess that's a plus."

"You don't know how they're made?"

"No, I'm sorry. Kin are created through a certain type of natural selection, be it genetic or mystical. There are arguments on that. The Sect pass it down through a bloodline, in families. Like in legend, the Sallow are made, but not how you think. Nobody really knows anything about the Vacant, and I personally just don't know much about the Throng."

"Okay."

I took one of my hands off the wheel and grabbed hers. "You're going to be okay."

"I don't want to become someone else, you know. Psychic powers and purple hair are one thing, but I still want to be me."

"Ah, gotcha."

"What?"

"Keegan, I was criminal scum before I became Kin in my early twenties. I did a stint in prison before I even met Rosenthal. When I did meet Rosenthal, I pretty much thought he was hiring me to kill someone."

"Oh."

"I don't think becoming one of the Tribe intrinsically changes who you are inside. I think living life as a member of the Carrion Court does that."

Keegan pulled her hand away. "I want to be better than that. Stronger."

I know Throng are supposed to feed on belief, but Keegan made me believe.

"If anyone can do that, it's you," I said.

CHAPTER 38

KELSEY

Back in the shack, I peered at the Sheffields and tried to decide my next move. With Jeff gone that was one less person to help on the hunts, and if I understood correctly, I would have uninvited company shortly. A Kin and a Throng. Something had to be done to boost my power, to increase the fear. I had an idea, but it was reckless.

My dad hadn't left yet. He was worried about me and wanted to take the day off work. We still had to figure out what to tell the family. Grandma wouldn't care, but I didn't think we could trust my mom. She was too volatile, and worse, probably let it slip to Tessa.

I decided I needed my dad, but not in the way he had imagined.

"Hey," I called out to him.

"What's up, sweetheart?"

Mike Radu strolled into the shack, immune to the horrific sight. He had grown up serving in a Sect abattoir and accepted it as part of reality. Bloodshed was part of his blood.

"Jeff had to go, but it doesn't come without repercussions," I said.

"I reckon so."

"I still have a ways to go to finish what I started here, and I don't know if I can achieve that that in the time frame set before me. At least not with the way we've been doing things. I know a way to kickstart things up a few notches, but it's risky as hell."

"A hunt?" asked my dad.

"No, something different. The town is already on edge with deaths and missing people, but this would set it off. Saturate it with fear. That fear would be drawn directly into the ves... into Ruby. It's one of those Hail Mary passes. I'd probably only need four or five people to feed on after that."

He frowned. "Hell, who all needs to die?"

"That's the good part, Ted's already dead," I replied, pointing to the corpse over my shoulder. "The bad part? There's a very good chance we're going to get caught."

I laid it all out for him. As far as Mike Radu was concerned it wasn't that much riskier than some of our kidnapping schemes. He made a few tweaks to the plan that I hadn't thought of and tightened it up. My dad was damn good at this kind of logistics.

So, we got to it.

Ted was removed from his shackles and mutilated a little bit more. I completely took off his lower jaw and all of his fingers except for his thumbs. There I sliced off the prints. Sure, they could DNA eventually, but I knew that actually took weeks, it not months, and that was if he was even in the system. This would be over by then. Besides, good 'ol Ted looked even more nightmarish now than he did before.

I painted a series of symbols all over his naked body with a paste I had in storage. It's a Sect creation of animal scat, herbs, oils, and curdled milk. Powerful stuff. I imbued Ted as a proxy for Pith, and a conduit of the vessel. It was a complicated and harrowing process, one that took me hours.

While I was doing that, my dad had retrieved one of the stolen vehicles in our garage. It was a van we had taken off a family. He had tinted the window already months ago, but now he was drilling holes into the body to fasten eyehooks to the interior. From the eyehooks were connected lengths of thin chain, enough to hold Ted in place. He had to be presentable. All the rear seats had been removed to make space for the tableau. Finally, because you never know when you'll need it, I had drained almost a half-gallon of blood from one of my playthings as a lark. I'm glad I had found a use for it. The container was going to sit ready until the very last moment.

It was almost dusk when they we were ready to go. My dad demanded to drive the van, and although I fought him on it, he held firm. I'd drive behind him. I wasn't happy about it, but I relented.

I followed, growing increasingly nervous as we made our way into town. I was worried someone would see through the tint or notice the tiny points of the eyehooks drilled through the van's body. I worried cops would randomly pull him over or he'd blow a tire. But none of that happened. Instead he made it all the way to the parking lot of Ennis's most popular restaurant, an Italian joint right in the middle of a busy strip mall.

Parking down in front of the sporting goods store, I could see him get out, walk around to the back of the van, and slightly open the back doors. Casually, my dad walked away from the van and towards me. There was nobody around, no one in sight. Dear fucking Pith, I think we had done it.

My dad jumped in the car next to me, smiling. "Well?"

"Holy shit, I think we pulled it off!"

"I knocked over the can of blood right before I got out. I think there was more in there than you thought."

"That's okay, doesn't matter."

He leaned back. "Now what?"

"Let's wait for a bit."

It didn't take long, maybe twenty minutes.

Two couples came out of the restaurant, heading to their cars. Laughing and smiling. I already knew. Sure enough, you could see one of the women smelled something. Squinting her nose, she gestured at the van to her boyfriend or husband. He said something and kept moving. Maybe she noticed the doors were open, maybe the blood had begun to trickle out. All that matters is that she opened the doors.

I could hear the screams from where I was sitting like she was standing beside me.

"Okay," I said. "We can go now."

CHAPTER 39

DANIEL

E nnis, Ohio. There wasn't much to it. A basic grid formation of a town with the river to one side and the foothills of the Appalachians to the other. The highway ran along the river and we came in from the north, entering to see an abandoned factory. Most of the windows were busted out, part of its façade covered in crude graffiti, and weeds creeping up in the cracked parking lot, it appeared a quintessential example of a rustbelt town.

Further in, we found more activity. There were a lot of police around for such a small town. ECPD, County Sheriff, and a few unmarked black SUV's that I didn't want to think about. Something was undoubtedly going down. I could tell Keegan had noticed it, too.

"What do you want to do?" she asked.

"Let's get breakfast, see what we can find out."

I picked another chain restaurant and pulled into the parking lot. There hadn't been many options. A number of cars sat out front, including those belonging to the local authorities. I considered how to play this.

"Can you read any thoughts from here?" I asked Keegan.

"Nah, too far away."

"Are you up for trying to go inside?"

She bit her lip and nodded. It was obvious she wasn't thrilled about the idea. I don't know if it was because there were police inside or because there were so many people, but she got out of the car and began walking. I rushed to catch up with her.

No one even gave us a second glance when we entered. No one cared. That was a major bonus in our favor. I was hoping we wouldn't have to deal with racist shitheads here. Either there weren't any or they were too preoccupied. I ordered us two breakfast sandwiches and two coffees, then discreetly scanned the room while I waited for our food. There were four ECPD cops and three regular customers. I went to make a comment to Keegan, but realized she was rubbing her forehead.

"You okay?" I asked.

"A lot of people in here, lots of noise in my head."

"See if you can just concentrate on the cops."

"Yeah."

We got our food and I snagged us a spot closer to the back, away from the kitchen. That seemed to help. Proximity was definitely a factor. I had noticed her hair gleamed slightly more purple than it had when we walked in, but I hoped nobody else would notice.

"They found a body in a van," whispered Keegan between bites. "Mutilated really bad. Occult stuff."

"Where?"

"Right here in town, parking lot of a strip mall."

I took a sip of my coffee and peered out the window. "Tribes don't leave bodies, especially not like that. I can't imagine it's unrelated though."

"Pretty much the whole town knows about it and are freaking out. A bunch of people saw the body before the cops arrived."

"Maybe to throw everyone off, including the Court?"

"I don't know, they're all freaked out."

The whole situation had me perplexed. After our little group discussion at Rosenthal's, it seemed likely that one of the Tribes in the Carrion Court was behind this. Sure, we hadn't deduced a how or why, but couldn't shake that idea. Theories starting swirling in my head. Could there be a rogue faction within the Court, a cabal of Throng, Vacant, and others working together? Could there be a secret sixth Tribe no one had ever known about? Could the humans actually know about us, and this be their strike against us?

"Daniel," Keegan said, her hand coming across the table to grip mine. "Your thoughts are screaming in my head. Calm down. All of that is incredibly doubtful."

"Sorry, I'm having a hard time processing this," I replied, squeezing her hand back.

"Let me ask you this? Who would benefit the most from dropping off a nightmare in the middle of a small town?"

It was the way she worded it. It made perfect sense.

"The Sect. They feed on fear."

Keegan smiled. "That's kind of what I was thinking."

"But they have to feed individually on their victims, up close and personal."

She shrugged. "Are you sure? They're witches. There're occult symbols all over the body. Maybe this is a special circumstance or something. It's not like everything recently has been normal."

"God damn it. You know, maybe we shouldn't indoctrinate everyone into the ways of the Carrion Court. Your out-of-the-box thinking is liable to solve this entire thing."

She beamed back at me. "I am very wise, I know."

We finished our food and began to leave. As we were existing, Keegan smiled at the youngest officer on the ECPD and he blushed. I was happy to know she could turn other men to goo. Back outside I stood by the car trying to formulate a plan.

"What's up?" she asked.

"Gimme a second."

Chances are we were in the right town, given the coordinates and the dead body. Given Keegan's hypothesis on the situation, I was willing to bet our target was indeed a Sect. Or a coven of them. How much area were we talking? Not much, the town wasn't even three miles across from its limits. Add in township, you had maybe ten or fifteen square miles of area to cover. I could cover the town's amount of space in a night in my wendigo form, but I wasn't about to try that with agitated cops afoot, and the township was too big. No, we were going to have to try something different.

"Hey Keegan."

"Yeah?"

"I have a plan you're gonna hate."

INTERLUDE 4

I t was something straight out of a horror movie, almost unreal. The whole area had been closed off, all of the strip mall's parking lot and even a couple of the stores along with the restaurant. The ECPD were in attendance with State Police watching their every move and a handful of FBI lurking around. The BCI&I had yet to take the body out of the van, still photographing every inch and seeking out any tiny forensic clue.

Hayward stood off to the side, out of the way and grumbling to Kenyon. They hadn't seen this coming. The arrival of this body had significantly changed things and altered the course of the investigation. The two officers would be lucky to be kept in the loop.

"Seventy-nine, are you at primary scene?" squawked Hayward's radio.

"Affirmative Dispatch,"

"Captain Long request you remain there until he arrives. "

"Copy."

Kenyon glanced over at him. "I wonder what that's about?"

"McVay has been too busy playing politics to yell at us, so I guess It's Long's job."

A few minutes later a squad car pulled up and a tall, handsome African American man with graying hair stepped out of the driver's seat. From the passenger seat, a striking woman with olive skin, blue eyes, and black hair got out. She was wearing a pantsuit and carrying a satchel. She sneered at the van in obvious disgust.

It took Hayward a few seconds to piece it together. "Dr. Wertz?"

It snapped her attention back. "Yes, I'm sorry. Dr. Constance Wertz. Please, call me Connie."

"You said you had contacted an expert. Looks like she decided to stop by at the exact right time," said Long.

"I didn't know you were coming," said Hayward.

She shrugged. "Bowling Green University isn't that far away, and I haven't seen Jen in forever. Plus, everything you told me was intriguing. I have to admit, I didn't expect to walk into this."

"This is new," offered Kenyon.

"Well, I know forensics has probably already taken things apart but I'd like to help however I can."

The officers exchanged glances.

"Everything is still in there," said Hayward. "Including the body. It's bad. The most brutal thing I've ever seen. Maybe you should wait for photographs."

She sighed. "No, it won't be the same. I think I can handle it."

Kenyon looked over to Long. "Will State or the Feebs even allow it?"

Long grinned. "I'll get it through."

It took about forty-five minutes of explaining and bullshitting, and another twenty minutes of signing paperwork, but finally Connie was led to the van. Most of the forensic techs were pulled away, only Long, Hayward, Kenyon, and an unnamed FBI agent present with her. She took a deep breath as they started to pull away the barrier screen.

"You sure?" asked Hayward.

"Yes."

And there it all was. Connie paled and covered her mouth. Hayward thought she was going to throw up, and began to move towards her, but she gestured for him to stay back. She breathed hard, in and out through her mouth three times, and looked back up to the visceral insanity.

"Okay," she said, her voice a little shaky. "Subject is crudely bound in chains in the back of a van but displayed in a manner that is ritualistic in nature. Possibly sacrificial. There are numerous injuries on the body, too many to count without autopsy. Unable to determine exact cause of death without autopsy. Some injuries could have occurred postmortem."

She leaned in closer to the van. "There appears to be a great deal of blood of the floor of van. Doubtful it came from the subject. Single secondary subject? Collected from multiple other subjects? Appears that it was held in white container at front of van."

Connie almost began to climb in the van, and Hayward went to stop her, but the FBI agent touched his arm and shook his head. Hayward raised an eyebrow but saw that she had stopped short of touching anything. The detective realized the agent was recording all of it on a small audio recorder.

"The symbols. They are painted on the body and the interior of the van. I'm unsure of the substance, but it looks like mud or fecal matter mixed with other substances. The symbols themselves are unlike any I've ever seen, ever associated with ceremonial or primitive magic. This is not Wiccan, Cabbalism, Hoodoo or Enochian. This... isn't any other of the major traditions, but there's a pattern here, so it's not nonsense, not something cobbled together. This could be someone's version of Chaos Magick, but I doubt it – it's too structured."

She looked back at the assembled officers. "I have a Ph.D. in Cultural Anthropology, with a specialty in the occult. Not to brag, but I am one of the leading experts in the country on this sort of shit."

"And?" asked Hayward.

"I have no idea what the hell I'm looking at right now."

"Great."

"This be could Scientologists who took too much LSD for all I know. But I don't think that."

"What do you think?" asked the FBI Agent.

"Some new cult, one incredibly organized in both belief and membership, has popped up near Ennis. They're acting out their belief system, much to our misery. You may be dealing with a lot more of them than you initially thought."

"How many?" asked Hayward.

Connie let out a breath. "I don't know, anywhere from ten to fifty. I'm guessing at this point. It's definitely more than two or three people, let's put it that way. This is too systematic for simply a handful of believers. I'll say twenty people."

"But you think it's new, this cult?" asked the Agent.

"There would have been some record of them before, either their symbols or murders like this. The symbols have a runic quality to them, but it's definitely not from any Pagan origin. It's like someone was reinterpreting cuneiform in a more fluid manner. I don't think anyone has seen this before."

"Thank you, Dr. Wertz," the Agent said, stopping the recording. "We'll be in touch."

As the ECPD officers kept talking to Connie, the Agent strolled off past the van. He nodded to forensic tech and answered a quick question from one of his FBI partners there in Ennis. A little thing, checking on some paperwork. After that, he stepped over by one of the black SUV's and pulled out his phone. Dialing a number, he smiled.

"Yes, it's me. There's nothing to worry about. While the so-called expert didn't connect the incident to any pre-established human groups, she believes it's a new human cult of, get this, twenty or so people. Right? Yes. Yes, I'll keep an eye on things here and be ready on your say."

CHAPTER 40

KELSEY

That night after we got back from dropping off the van, things went sideways. I didn't pay much attention to my mom anymore except when she was screaming. That's to say, I didn't put much stock in her cognitive faculties these days. I didn't view her as an authority figure from a parental viewpoint, or even as Sect, from a magical perspective. While she needed fear on occasion, the magic had burnt out her sanity years ago, along with her ability to properly wield any kind of spellcasting. To me, she was little more than an irritation that shrieked and ate.

I underestimated her.

It was dark by the time my dad and I got home, parked the car, and shuffled into the house. I was hoping there might be some food ready, but the table was empty. Turning to see who was around, I was hurled across the room by an unseen force and pinned against the kitchen wall.

"Kelsey!" exclaimed my dad.

"What have you done!" bellowed my mom, hands up and controlling the magic.

I struggled against her hold, trying to break free. I was two feet off the ground, bound tight in an invisible grip. Her eyes were wide in madness, teeth bared like an animal's.

"Angie, let her go!" yelled my dad.

"We felt it, all the way up here! Whatever you did, you roped your dad into it, and endangered us all! No more!"

My grandma rolled her way into the room and winked at me. She didn't intervene, but nor did she help. I didn't know what to do. Consciousness was slowly fading as I heard my mom babble on more lunatic proclamations.

"They'll be no more of this nonsense in my house, do you hear me. My house, my rules! The elders will have to find another way, that's all. They'll understand."

I could hear my dad begging her to let me go. Tessa had appeared, crying beside my grandma. The old woman still had said nothing, she showed no real emotion.

"I'll be priestess of this clan again, not you, Kelsey. No more Pith for you, little girl."

That did it.

Energies drawn up from deep within the Carrion Cradle built up in me and exploded, obliterating the hold my mom had on me. The magic she was using backlashed onto to her, sending her flying into a china cabinet. Dazed, she moaned and raised her head to see me enveloped in a fog of black, shimmering stars. Pure Sect magic, the true essence of Pith.

"No," I said. "You are here to serve me for as long as I allow it, in Pith's name."

"Kelsey?" tried my mom.

"I am the priestess here, not you. Not any longer, and never again."

For a moment there was clarity. Then Angela Radu's face twisted in a scowl. "You will ruin this family."

"You did that years ago, mom."

I glanced over at my Grandma and raised an eyebrow but the old woman chuckled. "I knew you could do it. Your release wouldn't have amounted to dogshit had I done it for you."

What do you say to that?

I went over to Tessa who was sitting on the floor, wiping away her tears. She seemed okay, but I wanted to make sure. The dark stars had all faded, leaving me normal-Kelsey once more. Or so I thought. My little sister didn't flinch or anything when I knelt down beside her. She was far more well-adjusted than I ever had been.

"Are you alright?"

"Yeah, I guess," she replied. "What about you?"

"I'm fine. Sorry about all that."

My mom screeched something from across the room, but grandma told her to shut up.

"Where's Jeff?" Tess asked.

This was the moment. "Jeff's took a gig down river on a barge. Real good money. He won't be back for like a week."

Tessa snorted and gave a small smile. "If he doesn't get fired first."

"For real," I said, giving her a hug.

I faced my family and sighed. They deserved to know what was coming. It was dangerous, to all of them potentially.

"Listen, please. Yes, I performed a very risky ritual today in downtown Ennis. I had to. There is a Kin and Throng working together and they're on their way here right now, coming for us."

"What?" squawked my mom.

"If you don't believe me, ask grandma."

"It's true, bones told me, Pith confirmed it."

"I did the ritual in hopes that I can complete this whole thing before they arrive, so it doesn't matter. But I can't promise that. Honestly, Mom, I'm glad you're still so powerful, because you may have to help protect the family along with everyone else."

She gritted her teeth. "I have no problem doing that."

"Okay," I said. "Okay."

Everyone mused on these revelations for a bit while I pondered what to do next. My eyes fell on Tessa and it occurred to me what tonight would be perfect for. I didn't want another fight, so I was going to have to do this carefully.

My mom had pulled herself out the china cabinet and cleaned up. Wobbling back to her couch, she plopped down with my dad's help and was now ignoring everyone, but still throwing suspicious glares in every direction. Nothing appeared really wounded on her but her pride. I slowly walked over to the couch and knelt down in front of her, where she visibly stiffened.

"Mom, I want to take Tessa outside and talk to her about how to stay safe in the coming days. Show her places she can hide. I don't want to lose her like we did Ruby. Is that okay?"

She looked confused for a moment, then softened. "That's a damn good idea. You two go."

Of course, that's not want I was taking Tessa for.

"Where are we going?" I was asked as soon as we got on the porch.

We headed to the shack, where I showed her Lily. I explained that Lily was broken and in a catatonic state. I couldn't get fear out of her anymore even though she was still alive. Usually, I'd just kill her.

"But you need to start learning now," I said. "Before your Sect powers kick in."

"Oh, um... okay. So, what do I do?"

"Well, she's already quite damaged, but would you like to do?"

"Stab her in the neck?"

"No, that would kill her instantly. We can't have that."

"Right! Because if you wanted the fear, you'd wanna keep her alive!"

"Exactly. What instead?"

Lily began examining the tools, glancing back at Lily every so, often as if to confirm what it might do to her. I hopped up on one of the tables, found my cigarettes in the ceiling and lit one up. Eventually she settled on a melon baller and beamed up at me.

"How about one of those pretty eyes?"

"You're a chip off the 'ol block, kiddo."

CHAPTER 41

DANIEL

I climbed into the car with Keegan and we began driving around Ennis. Chances are we looked suspicious, but there was nothing that could be done about it. There was an initial plan that I was pretty sure wouldn't work, and a backup plan. The nuclear option, if you'd like.

"Anything?" I asked.

"Snippets of voices as we drive past, sure. Nothing out of the ordinary there. I'm not positive."

"I'm sensing a 'but' in there."

"There's something else," she said. "I felt it as soon as we got into town, but I didn't really know what I was experiencing. Hell, at first I thought it was just anxiety, but now I'm pretty certain it's something else."

"What?"

"I can't explain in, a quality in the air. No, that sounds dumb, too simple. Diffused in the air, merged with it. Like a blanket laying over top of the town, the people. Us."

This was problematic. Keegan had enough power to pick up on that something was manipulating the town but lacked the experience to deduce what was behind it. Another Throng might have been able to recognize such machinations instantly. Still, her discovery of this energy leads me to believe we were indeed in the right place.

We went around a few more blocks, hoping for any clues. Nothing. Almost three hours had been taken up cruising around Ennis, and I didn't think we could risk it anymore. Too many cop cars had been passed already.

I pulled into a gas station so, we could both use the rest room, and grab some snacks. Keegan made fun of me for eating like a child, with my beef jerky, Doritos, and energy drinks. I eyed her pumpkin seeds and tea and rolled my eyes. She knew I was smiling, though.

"We're going to that gazebo, aren't we?" she asked.

There went the smile. "Keegan, if you don't think you can do it, please say so."

"We don't have a choice," she said, getting back in the car.

While we were driving around, I had noticed a gazebo early on in what seemed to be the center of town. It was a small patch of lawn, with a few bushes and benches, roads on three sides with businesses on the fourth. Chances are it was the central point for festivals and parades. Fortunately, it was a few miles from where the body had been found so, no one was really paying much attention to it, Plus, it was in the opposite direction from the police station.

We might actually be left alone for fifteen minutes.

Most of the parking spaces around the gazebo area were empty, so I picked one. We took our food and headed towards it. Keegan linked her arm around mine and beamed up at me.

"Act casual," she said. "We're having a pleasant lunch in the gazebo."

"Right."

The white gazebo was larger than I thought, octagonal with benches built into the sides. Sitting down, I pounded the rest of my first energy drink and went to open the second, then thought better of it. Keegan was calmly sipping her tea and smirking at me.

"What?" I asked.

"Why are you nervous?"

"I worry about you."

"I know."

She shook out her arms, lowered her head, and said, "Let's do this."

I swear I could see the power radiate off Keegan Pembroke. Her hair turned purple almost immediately, as did her fingernails and lips. Her skin began to fade from a dark hue, glowing, transforming to a bubblegum pink. There were people around us, but they didn't see. But they began to fall, collapsing to the ground. Behind me, two cars crashed into to one another and a delivery van slammed into the side of a building. Keegan had gone almost completely pink; her glow was intensifying. From behind her closed eyelids, light started to leak out.

"Keegan, enough!" I reached out and grabbed her. "Come back!"

She instantly snapped back, a slight purple hue back to her hair.

"Hey, hi... um, that was weird," her words slightly slurred.

"Are you okay?"

"What? Oh yeah, I'm fine. That was intense. I felt everybody."

"I don't think you should do that again."

Keegan smiled. "Won't have to. I'm pretty sure I know where they are."

"Really?"

"It's hard to explain, but yeah. They know what's going on, and I'm almost positive they're from a Tribe because their minds are different, like yours, but... I don't know what they are. Sorry. Too many minds to get much detail."

"It's okay. I don't suppose you know how many?"

Keegan grimaced. "More than one, less than ten?"

"Fair enough."

Everything was getting back to normal around them. People getting up off the ground, drivers exiting their vehicles. It was time to go. I was going to try to convince Keegan to act like she needed help walking, but it turned out she was a bit wobbly anyhow. I helped her to the car and we got out of there before any of the authorities arrived.

Back at the gas station, I got her some coffee and ibuprofen. She took both and stretched in the parking lot while I called Rosenthal and updated him. He still hadn't heard back from Mayumi and Koller, but that wasn't out of the ordinary and assumed everything was going to plan. I hoped that was the case and hung up.

Keegan walked over, looking refreshed. "Now what?"

"You tell me?"

"We go up," she said, pointing to the massive hillside that overlooked Ennis.

"Okay."

CHAPTER 42

KELSEY

That morning.

Lily was dead. Tessa had done well learning how to play with her - stabbing, burning, slicing, breaking, etc. At some point I had fallen asleep on the floor, leaving my sister to her own entertainment. I don't know when Lily finally died, but at some point, Tessa had painted her face up like a clown's. I sat there with bloody straw in my hair, staring at this, pondering if the makeup could have been possibly done after death and why.

Whatever. My family was the definition of eccentric. I suppose I didn't expect such oddities from Tessa.

I went to my trailer to get a shower. Everything about me was a mess. Falling asleep in the shack was a stupid move on multiple levels. I'd never done that before. I wanted to scold myself for the act, but the way I saw it, this would all be over soon. Instead I got cleaned up and concentrated on the future.

There needed to be another hunt. Unfortunately, this was where I ran into some hurdles. Jeff was dead and my dad was at work. My mom and grandma were no help for their own reasons. Tessa might aid in her own ways, but she really wasn't ready. Not now, not with all the cops buzzing around the present I had left them downtown. That left it all up to me.

I had an idea, but I would have to be bold. And damn lucky.

I slipped on a pair of black yoga pants and an off the shoulder pink tee. No bra, of course. Found some boots that didn't quite fit that I'd stolen off a victim. I thought they looked cool. Makeup on, hair down. Checking myself out in the mirror, I almost looked good. Definitely not pregnant, at least.

It was about 10:30 when I snagged one of the cars to drive down into Ennis, maybe a little later. I pulled up at the dollar store and saw Liz McCreary's SUV parked off to the side. I parked next to it. Yes, I may have been casually stalking her in my free time the last couple of weeks.

I took a deep breath and walked in the doors. She stood there, beautiful as before. For a moment, my plan faltered. Then she glanced over at me, a war of emotions on her face.

"Hey," she said.

"Hey," I replied. "Um, can I... I wanted to apologize. Sincerely."

"Oh."

"My life is shit. For a few seconds I was happy, and then I was reminded. And I blamed you for that."

Liz smiled. "Kelsey, damn."

"When do you get off? I just want to talk."

"11:30."

"I'll be by your car." I said.

"Sounds good."

I left the store shaking. I hadn't meant to say all that. I had a different speech planned. Similar, but not that. That was too honest. Not just to her, but myself. I hated that I had said those words out loud, that someone knew how weak I was. She was definitely going to have to die now.

I sat in my car for nearly an hour before Liz came out. The curvy ginger had unbuttoned more of her shirt again. I tried to push those feelings down, ignore them. She slid into the passenger side of my car and began to light up a cigarette, then gasped.

"Oh, I'm... uh."

"It's okay. I'm still trying to quit. Gimme one."

We both lit up and puffed in silence for a minute.

"So, if you don't mind me asking, what happened to Jeff? I thought you two were together?"

Good, something I'd planned for. "Jeff is fucking idiot. He can't hold down a job and he was never someone I was interested in long-term. He's not really in the picture anymore, my choice."

"Gotcha."

"You've got to understand, I love this baby, and I'm happy for its existence, but everything else in my world is pretty miserable. I do what I do for her."

"Oh, you know it's a girl already?"

"Yeah."

"You have names yet?"

I smiled. No one had asked me that question except for Jeff, and funny enough, he loved the name.

"Jade. It's a play on my older sister's name."

"Didn't she move to Florida or something?" asked Liz.

I sighed. That was the cover story we all had come up with.

"Maybe you could move down there with her?"

Her eyes only showed concern. She actually cared. Inside, I think my heart was breaking a little. Here was someone I had thought about for years, perhaps even potentially had some sort of future with. But what kind of future? Living in another rundown house that was little more than a shed in the dying town of Ennis, raising my daughter as a Sect in the shadow of the Carrion Court? The fear of persecution because I was an "other?" – a witch, a lesbian, a single mother. That's what this current world offered. It all had to be torn down and burnt away, starting fresh was the only way forward for our society.

"Liz," I said. "In some other life."

"Huh?"

"Dashoon."

She was out. She'd be out for a good six hours. I put the car in drive and pulled out of the parking lot. Heading out of Ennis, I knew one of those last lines had been crossed. There were still a few more to go, those barriers I'd have to overcome before Pith would arrive and remake the world.

It would all be worth it.

It had to be.

CHAPTER 43

DANIEL

The car twisted and turned for a while on the outskirts of downtown Ennis. Keegan had a general idea of what direction we needed to go, but that didn't mean the roads cooperated. We knew we needed to go uphill and mostly to the south. It was becoming clearer to her the closer we got.

When we left the downtown area and went under the highway it seemed equivalent to crossing over to the "wrong side of the tracks." Over here, houses were even more rundown, with broken out windows and shingles falling off into unkept grass. Rusting vehicles sat on blown out tires, guarded by near feral dogs that barked as we passed. A child sat in the dirt and gawked at us open mouthed, his hands filled with mud.

This wasn't just a few homes, all of them were like this. Poverty and despair made manifest. Keegan said something to me, but I didn't hear her. There were piles of garbage outside of one house, simply discarded over time, as if the front yard were an acceptable place to toss dirty diapers. Baffling.

"Hey, turn right here," she said.

Grumbling to myself, I did. I was having an inner conflict over everything I had seen on the drive, concentrating on the house with the garbage for some reason. My true self, the Kin in me, wanted to go back and slaughter every living person in there. They wanted to live like animals, let them be killed the same. However, the part of me that Keegan had touched and awakened, this better part, felt empathy. This second side wanted to help them, raise them up, and show them there was hope.

I didn't like it, being pulled in two directions like that. Sure, a person could have competing opinions on a subject, but this was far more disconcerting. At this point, I wasn't sure how I even really felt, and that was potentially dangerous.

Keegan frowned at me. "You okay?"

"I don't know."

"What's up?"

I figured she can read my mind anyways, so what the hell. "I'm... I'm pretty sure I have feelings for you, but I'm not sure how genuine they are, because you're a Throng. And that upsets me. And because of those feelings, I think you influence my thoughts without realizing it."

"Well," she said, bringing her knees up in the seat. "If you had the presence of mind to tell me all that, let alone think it, my wicked Throng magic can't be that powerful."

That made me laugh. "I suppose you're right."

"In any case, we can't worry about it now, last right turn here I believe. It's practically glowing up ahead."

We were on a dirt road now, likely someone's driveway. It wove around for almost a mile at an incline, thick woods and underbrush on both sides. It was worn down quite well, and relatively wide, lending me to think that while it was never well cared for, the driveway had been around for some time. Up ahead, I could make out a structure through the trees,

The land flattened out, and we pulled the car through into the clearing. A large house out stood there, badly in need of repair. Along with it was some kind of rectangular shed, a trailer, and a massive open front garage holding almost a dozen vehicles. I don't know what I was expecting, but this hadn't been it.

"Are you sure this is the place?"

Keegan rubbed her temples and made a face. "Yeah, I'm sure. It's giving me a headache just being here."

I got out of the car and looked around, Keegan doing the same. There was no one here. I had assumed we'd come barreling into an army, and I'd have to leap from the Mercedes fighting. I got it into my head that we'd find some kind of church built up here, some insane structure. Or at least a headquarters befitting the absolute shitstorm befalling the Carrion Court. Nope. It was basic residential property that looked a step or two above what I had seen below.

I threw up my hands. "I don't know, do you want to investigate the house?"

"Makes sense, I guess," said Keegan. "That or the weird shed."

"Yeah, probably nothing but..."

That's when we heard the chanting.

I started to turn to see two women on the porch to house, an elderly one in a wheelchair and the morbidly obese middle aged one. Words churned from their mouths, accented with complicated hand gestures. Even from the distance I stood, the malice in their faces was apparent.

Two steps were all I managed to pull off before I went down on one knee. Using every bit of strength, I turned my head towards Keegan. She was flat on the ground, sobbing. I tried to call to The Mist but couldn't. I couldn't move enough to commune with it, bond with it. Sect, there was no doubt about it.

Their magic kept at me, trying to force me down. I fought against it, but I could feel my ankle starting to snap. Roaring, I went into the grass, held there against my will. Seething with pain, the only good thing was from my vantage point I could still see Keegan and she could see me. I wanted to tell her that everything would be okay, even if that was a lie, but I couldn't move my mouth at this point.

I was probably on the ground for a few minutes when I heard the sound of another engine pulling up. It cut out, and feet stomped across the ground over to me. Out of my peripheral vision, I managed to see a teenage girl scowling down at me.

"God damn it," she said.

CHAPTER 44

KELSEY

So, I was climbing up the hill in the car with Liz beside me, thinking up all the wonderful ways I was going to entertain myself, and I may have been daydreaming a bit. Things were getting tense, and I simply wanted a day to myself with Liz. I didn't feel like that was too much to ask. Instead I had to slam on the breaks, almost bashing the front end of my car into the back end of some fancy Mercedes. That pulled me out of my fantasy really quick and I realized what was going on around me.

Leaping from the car, I immediately assumed we were all in far more peril than what we were. Turned out, not that perilous a situation. I felt a surge of pride for my mom and grandma. They had done it. Without a doubt this was the Kin and the Throng. Not only could I sense it in my blood, their otherness, but who the hell else would randomly show up here?

My mom shot me a look, clenched teeth and bulging eyes. She was barely holding it together. I had the hand it to her for holding out this long.

"God damn it," I said, before racing back to the car.

My dad had been smart enough to conceal weapons of all sorts in the vehicles we drove, nothing we'd necessarily get in trouble for having, but items that could be useful. I pulled an incredibly sharp hunting knife out from under the driver's seat and rushed back to the Kin face down on the ground. He growled something at me, but I didn't pay attention. Instead, I slit up the back of the shirt exposing skin and proceeded to carve a symbol there before infusing it with magic. Hopping over to the Throng girl, I did the same while she sobbed.

"Okay, let them go!" I yelled.

The Kin spun on the grass, ready to lunge, but a look of confusion dropped over him. I pulled the Throng girl up against me, the knife to her throat.

"Old Sect spell. Neither of you have access to your Tribe magic. Basically, you're both human now."

The Kin smiled. "I can still kill you even if I'm human."

"Not before I open this one up, and I have a feeling you won't do that."

The throng choked out a name. It sounded like "Daniel."

"Daniel is it? And what's your name, princess?"

"Don't," he said.

"Hush, Daniel. The girls are talking."

"Keegan," whispered the Throng. "My name is Keegan."

"That's an interesting name, I've never known a 'Keegan.' Of course, I've never a met a Throng, either. My name's Kelsey."

"For fuck's sake, stop playing around!" my mom screeched from the porch.

"Now what?" asked Daniel.

I shifted my stance behind Keegan. "Now I'm going to carefully lead Keegan into that building behind me. You're going to follow. Too fast, I kill her. Too slow, I kill her. Anything stupid, I kill her. You're going to chain yourself up, then I'm going to chain Keegan up. Then I'm going to finish what I started."

"Which is what?" asked Keegan.

"Eh, we'll get to that."

Slowly I walked the Throng backwards towards the shack. I could tell the Kin was ready to attack at the first chance he got, but this wasn't the first time I'd had somebody at knifepoint. The whole procession took longer than I would've liked, but we got there. Pretty little Keegan did not react well we she saw the shack, but the blade pressed firmer against her throat shut her up.

The Kin was easily the biggest threat, but between the symbol and the girl, I felt he was relatively neutralized. Positioned against the wall I had him raise his arms and place them into the shackles attached there. I was intimately familiar with every inch of the devices in the building, so I would know if he tried to fake the manacles locking or any such nonsense. Surprisingly, he did everything as instructed, leaving the last lock for me. I snapped it closed without a word.

I was appraising Keegan while I bound her next to the Kin. Against my better judgment, I had to admit she was attractive.

Still, she was dangerous. It was strange, though. I don't know much about Throng. Out of the three of us, she looked somehow "more than human." Not even that she was pretty, but some other quality. It was almost unnerving.

Sadly, there would be no time to amuse myself with the Throng girl. I had Liz still in the car. That would take up most of today. I kept telling myself that as I left the shack, Daniel whispering to Keegan beside him, Whatever, there was nothing they could do. No, no... everything had turned around. Smooth sailing from here.

My mom was screaming on the front porch.

"How dare you allow these strangers come onto my land! These threats! It's gonna end, girl! You hear me!"

I ignored her and walked over to the Mercedes to check the ignition for keys. Jackpot. Getting in, I moved the car out of the way so, my dad could pull in later. Chances are the vehicle would have to be dumped. Something like it was probably going to have a GPS.

"You listen to me when I talk to you! You listen and you obey!"

I had walked back up to the car with Liz in it. I was about to climb in when my mom started to take a waddling step off the porch in my direction. Spinning, I marched towards her, bellowing back.

"No, you listen! I am the priestess of this coven, and you're just a lunatic old woman who contributes nothing to this family anymore except for being a burden. If you stand in my way or defy me one more time, Angela Radu, I will kill you. I will orchestrate your end in the name of Pith."

My mom fumbled back and fell onto the porch. Without saying another word, I got into the car and drove it down to the shack. There was work to be done.

CHAPTER 45

DANIEL

There was no access to The Mist. Whatever those two on the porch had done had first made it impossible to move, to shift my body enough to physically call it forth, and now it was like there was some sort of block on the magic itself. Made sense, considering we were dealing with Sect. I assumed it was connected with whatever that girl had carved into our backs. My shirt hung in tatters around my chest, and I could feel the blood drying on my back. It didn't really hurt anymore and I was more pissed than anything else. I had been so, stupid. From the beginning of this investigation, I had been stupid, but being around Keegan made me a complete fucking idiot.

Keegan. She was not handling this well at all. She was still crying, hanging in her shackles seemingly defeated. Every time she moved, she winced in pain. That girl, Kelsey, had ripped off her flannel and cut up the back of her shirt like mine, sliced right through her bra strap. It reasoned that whatever was carved in my back was carved into hers, or something similar. Her hair had lost all of its purple hue.

"Keegan, we'll get out of this," I whispered. "It's going to be okay."

No reply.

"We'll figure something out. Besides, I called Rosenthal. He'll get here."

Nothing.

"Keegan, everything is…"

"There's a dead body on display back there," she said.

"What?"

"In the back," she said, her voice shaking. "There's a dead body strung up."

We were interrupted by a car pulling down by the entrance. A car door slammed, and all we could hear was movement. Then the Sect girl entered dragging another young woman. I wasn't sure how to respond to this, so I said nothing. Keegan remained silent as well. There was a vertical beam the new victim was attached to by her hands and feet. Unconscious the whole time, it was a struggle the Sect seemed to enjoy.

The Sect girl, Kelsey, was not what I had been expecting. Tall and slender, quite pretty with dyed black hair and fair skin, she couldn't have been older than eighteen or twenty. Examining her closer, I was pretty sure she was in her first trimester of pregnancy.

"See, that's nice," said Kelsey, admiring her handiwork.

"So, a Sect and her family have become serial killers. That's... boring," I said.

"Oh, you think?"

I attempted a shrug. "You're using too much magic and it's screwing everybody up. Still boring. I came here looking for some epic cult or a secret sixth Tribe."

Kelsey smiled and glanced over at Keegan. She must've caught Keegan eyeing the corpse in the back of the building, because she started laughing. Walking back there, Kelsey gestured around the room.

"Do you like what we've done with the place? I see you've noticed my sister back there. Yeah, that's Ruby. But it won't be Ruby for much longer."

Keegan made a small noise. "Your sister? But why?"

"I'm not going to give away all the plan, c'mon. But since you made it this far, I'll tell you this – I'm tapping into the magic, all the magic, which is why it's affecting the other Tribes. And once I'm successful, it won't matter anymore."

"You're killing thousands, possibly millions." I said.

"So? I don't care. It'll be worth it."

"What will?" pleaded Keegan.

"Not telling."

I couldn't help but laugh. "You do realize you are almost completely out of time. I called the Kin elders from town. They know where we are. This is not a ploy; this is not a lie. You may have stopped the two of us, you may even kill us, but you can't stop an army from the Carrion Court."

Kelsey had turned from me. I could see her rubbing her belly. Yep, she was definitely pregnant. She didn't appear angry or scared, just thinking. Calculating. Before, part of me believed this Sect girl was simply insane or a child over her head. Watching her in those few moments, I began to think differently.

"I agree, time's almost up," said Kelsey. "But I have a bit more time than you might think. And I'm almost finished."

She sauntered over to Keegan and began to play with her hair. Keegan stiffened as Kelsey began to kiss her neck and run her hands up and down her arms. I wasn't sure what the hell was happening. Then Keegan began to scream.

"Stop, stop! What the hell are you doing?"

Kelsey pulled away, blood all over her mouth. It was blood from Keegan's ear, where she had bitten Keegan's earlobe off. Leaning back in, she began to chew on the ear as her hand slid up the front of Keegan's shirt.

I thrashed in my chains. "Leave her the fuck alone!"

As Keegan was about to scream again, Kelsey went in for what I thought was a kiss. It wasn't. Instead the Sect inhaled deeply and some type of smoke like substance billowed out of Keegan. Keegan collapsed back against the wall, alive but exhausted.

Kelsey staggered back. "My god, I've never tasted anyone like that. I need to start hunting Throng."

She disappeared back towards the corpse, but I was too busy trying to tend to Keegan to pay much attention to whatever was going on there. She wasn't even crying, but eyelids fluttered in a worrying manner. I tried calling her name, but she wasn't responding.

Kelsey was coming to end, that much I knew. I wanted to be the one to do it. I just hoped her death came soon enough.

CHAPTER 46

KELSEY

L eft to their suffering, it was time to season the vessel. Over at Ruby, I breathed into her open mouth, filling her with the Throng's fear. She had tasted beautiful, delicious. I wanted her again, even though I knew she wouldn't be able to provide yet. It made me wonder about the Kin and what kind of flavor he would have. Honestly, I was concerned I wouldn't be able to harvest any fear from him. I doubted Daniel had any fear of pain or death, but perhaps he did fear for Keegan. I was going to have to test that.

Sitting down on the dirt in front of Ruby, I peered up at her and considered my next move. Obviously, Liz was going to go along with Keegan. I'd get what I could out of Daniel. Would that be enough? It was like I was filling up an invisible bucket with measuring cups of an unknown size. I was confident I was almost full, but now I was running against the clock. Would three more victims do it? Would it take five? Would I even know until I had finished?

Ruby didn't look any different from the day we had prepared her with the elders. There was no rot, only magic, but that magic hadn't changed. No indication of what was occurring inside. All I had to go on was what Pith was telling me, and I had to believe him.

I had nothing else.

There needed to be more fear. There was no way I could come this close and be stopped. The town was gripped by terror, all of it seeping up into the vessel, but it still wasn't enough. A few more victims, some last mainline hits.

My dad was going to have to help. Probably Tessa, too. I didn't like the idea of the latter, but it couldn't be helped. Passing my captives, Keegan had started coming around and Daniel growled something at me. Liz was still out, limp on the ground. I'd get back to her later. I had hoped to spend some quality time with her, but I wasn't sure if I'd get the chance now.

The tow truck was parked by the house, so I was hoping I could snag my dad and Tessa and be off before there was too much of a commotion. I should've known better. I could hear the screaming as soon as I set foot on the porch.

"We were attacked!" shrieked my mom. "They would have killed us, killed the whole family! You would've come home to find your wife and babies dead, Mike!"

"What would you expect me to do against a wendigo? A Kin and a Throng together?"

"Defend us!"

I stepped into the house to see my mom's whole-body quivering in delusional, self-righteous anger. She had my dad back up against the wall, a finger in his face. My grandma sat in her wheelchair, shaking her head.

My mom shook her fists in the air. "We were defenseless!"

"Bullshit," I said. "You and grandma were the ones who stopped them."

Grandma barked out a laugh. I could see Tessa peeking out from the steps. My dad sighed.

Angela Radu spun on me. "Traitor! You're a traitor to this family. Don't think I don't know what you did to Jeff! You'll betray us all for your..."

That was it. I realized right then what I had to do.

With a burst of power, I sliced my hand flat through the air. Her knees instantly shattered, toppling her over with a wail. My dad went to help her, but I sent him scurrying back with a look. She tried to crawl, but at her size, it was nearly impossible.

"Angela Radu, as priestess of this coven, I find you guilty of heresy in the name of Pith."

My Grandma cackled. "Heresy, nice. An oldie, but a goodie."

"You are a heretic, you are a burden, and you are worthless. You are worthless except for one reason. Dad and Grandma have no fear, Tessa has potential. You? You fear everything. I'm going to feed that fear to Pith."

My dad began quietly weeping, while grandma simply nodded. I hear the backdoor slam as Tessa ran outside, that was fine, this was probably too much for her.

And my mom? She kept screaming through her tears.

"Don't you dare, you little whore! You obey me, I demand it!"

I realized now it had always been coming to this, every day between us leading up to this moment. Part of my concentration was holding her in place, tapping down her own magic, while I walked into the kitchen. She still had fight in her, even if she had her knees blown out. I found two large knives and carried them back into the living room.

"You'll pay for this, you'll all pay! I'll kill all of you!"

I stepped over to my dad and kissed him on the cheek. "I'm so, so sorry."

He smiled at me through tears. "She's been dead for years."

"You piece of shit loser, you fucking slave!"

In one quick motion, I plunged the first knife down into one of her hands and impaling it into the floor. As she screamed and tried to go for it, I grabbed her other hand and did the same. With her bulk and busted knees, she was effectively trapped.

She looked up at me from the dirty hardwood floor, her face was trembling. Perhaps some switch had flipped once more, a realization that she couldn't yell away an oncoming storm. Even though I could perceive traces of sanity in her eyes, it didn't matter. I could see fear, too.

"Kelsey, please."

"Not too much longer, mom."

CHAPTER 47

DANIEL

K eegan was finally back and semi-functional, talking at least although she was pretty sluggish. She seemed okay minus the ear, but I could tell she was traumatized. I could shake off an attack like that, but she was struggling.

That was when the redhead girl woke up.

"Wha... what the fuck? Where am I?"

"Quiet, calm down," I said. "You've been captured, just like us."

"Let me go! Let me out!" she screamed.

I shook the chains. "We're locked in here, too!"

Her eyes darted around, and I could see her piecing things together in her head. Taking in the sight of Keegan and I, the room we were in, and what she could glimpse outside the open doors. I was about to ask her some questions when something obviously clicked and her whole demeanor changed.

"That bitch," she said. "I'll fucking kill her."

"Who?" I asked.

"Kelsey Radu."

"You know her?"

"We went to high school together. We... it doesn't matter. Yeah, I thought we were friends."

Keegan rose her head. "She's responsible for all the murders in the area."

The girl went white. "Shut up."

"What's your name?" I asked.

"Liz."

"Liz, Kelsey isn't human."

"Yeah, this is all pretty twisted."

I smiled. "No, Kelsey is legitimately not human. She is a Sect, what is commonly known as a Witch. Her whole family is. They have magic and feed off fear. They've been trying to complete an insane ritual here in this building."

"The only thing insane is you, man."

"I'd tell you I'm a Wendigo and she's a Faerie, but that's not going to help my argument much."

"What's a Wendigo?"

I sighed. This wasn't going anywhere. I probably shouldn't have bothered, but I felt like this girl should know what we all were up against. Unfortunately, it looked like Liz was going to find out all too soon.

Kelsey came hurrying into the building with her cheeks puffed out, almost as if she were holding her breath. She ignored all of us completely, even Liz who immediately began hurling obscenities at her. The young Sect rushed to the back and climbed up to the corpse. From where I was shackled, I couldn't quite make out what she was doing.

"What's she doing?" I whispered to Keegan.

"I can't see."

After a couple of minutes, she came strolling back to the front, all smiles and rosy cheeks. Keegan and I stayed quiet as Liz continued to berate her, not grasping the danger she was in. I was about to say something when Kelsey kicked the girl in the leg. Hard. The girl squealed and teared up, her words cutting off.

"Liz, I used to fantasize about you," said Kelsey. "I mean for years, I thought about you. But I've come to realize you're just a distraction. Something that threatens to pull me away from my path, and I can't have that. After my goal is achieved, there will be others. So many others. Best to enjoy you as a means to an end now."

"What are you even talking about?" asked Liz through tears.

"I'm going to play with you and hurt you, drink up all your fear, and then kill you."

Liz began screaming again as Kelsey went and retrieved a small knife. Keegan and I watched as she cut away portions of the girl's clothing, giving Liz both kisses and cuts along the way. Occasionally the Sect would lick at the wound, tasting Liz's blood. Kisses and cuts, kisses and cuts. Despite this all, Liz fought through her tears.

I could feel Keegan beside me shaking. Even without any mental link, I knew she was terrified. Aghast. She didn't want to be subject to this, and even though I was no longer under her Throng influence, I was realized something. I would die before I would let this lunatic girl harm Keegan again. I didn't know when these feelings had become real or why, but they had. I would not watch her get violated in the same manner.

The rest of Liz's clothing was removed. Now naked, the young human merely stared up at Kelsey defiantly. I had to hand it to Liz, she was determined to make it difficult for the Sect. Kelsey didn't seem to notice, she was too busy gawking at Liz's body. I honestly thought she was going to start masturbating right there, but instead walked over and swapped out her tools. She grabbed a much smaller knife. Kelsey stomped over and went to work on Liz's right eye. We couldn't see much, but we could hear the screams.

Two bits of skin were tossed off to the side. Kelsey knelt down, one hand gripping Liz by the hair, the other clasping her left breast. Her mouth was on Liz's face. When she got up, blood was all over Kelsey's mouth, and the same blood poured from Liz's empty eye socket. Walking up to us, she opened to mouth to show the eye there before closing it and chewing.

Keegan screamed.

Liz moaned.

I shrugged.

Kelsey went back over to Liz and began to abuse her sexually, using the blood from her eye in creative ways. Even I thought it was ghastly, and I eat people. This went on for about ten minutes until Kelsey, Liz now weeping from one good eye, until she was yanked back and drained of her fear. I watched Kelsey take it back to the corpse, convinced that dead body was the key to everything.

She drained a bit of fear from Keegan again, but I didn't say anything. There was no point, Plus, she hadn't had to hurt her. It gave me more time to figure things out. Kelsey didn't bother trying to tap me, she knew better. All she'd be getting from me was rage.

Strangely, I watched as Kelsey applied some kind of salve to Liz's eye and bandaged it almost tenderly. This young Sect still baffled me, both her motives and her methods. She was definitely a sexual sadist, but I couldn't tell if she had a compulsion to kill or that was simply a means to an end. I pulled on my chains and thought about the magic these Sect were wielding. It was all about the magic.

Kelsey waved goodbye to me as she departed and I was left with two unconscious companions. I shifted in my chains and tried to nudge Keegan. Magic, I had to think about the magic.

CHAPTER 48

KELSEY

Back in my trailer, I collapsed onto my bed. To say the last few days had been chaotic would be an understatement. Hell, the last twelve hours. None of this was how I envisioned these last few days going. Too much stress and panic. Too much uncertainty.

At least I could smoke in my own home now.

Intellectually, I knew what the problem was. I was struggling between what I wanted and what I needed. What I wished to be done and what had to be done. None of those were lining up very well.

I knew that Keegan and Daniel needed to be kept alive long enough so I could extract fear from them. As much as possible. But their presence made me uneasy. They were a risk, and I longed to slit their throats and be done with them. I hated that such dangerous adversaries were perhaps my best shot at finishing the ritual.

As much as I wanted to hurry it along with them, I desperately wanted to draw my time out with Liz. Time was something I didn't have. I could have played with nothing but her skin for a week. Maybe after ruining every inch of her, she'd finally be out of my system.

Looking back, there were no regrets about my mom. Not on my part. I felt bad for my dad. Tessa still hadn't shown up again. That upset me more than anything. Was my little sister mourning her mother's passing in solitude, or was it something more than that? I didn't like to examine the idea that maybe she was afraid of me now. I wanted to go out and search for her, but I couldn't, not with everything happening here. Back at the house, grandma said not to worry, that Tessa had run these hills all her life. My dad hadn't seemed to care. I still didn't know what to think.

Part of me began to doubt all of it, wondering if I had made one colossal mistake.

I rubbed my belly and thought of my baby growing up in this life, going down to Ennis City Elementary School with hand-me-down shoes and family secrets like Tessa, Ruby, and I did. My mom screaming at family dinner about whatever lunacy had crept into her head and Jeff pawing at me under the kitchen table like a hormonal teenager. Growing decrepit and despondent on this hillside without ever leaving, without ever getting a chance to be more.

Not for this child. I'd kill the world and smile.

I had to stay strong, physically and mentally.

I knew my dad needed some time and my Grandma could see to herself. Hopefully, Tessa would come back if I stayed away from the house. I needed some food and rest. Not much on either account, a bare minimum would get me through.

I microwaved a hotdog and stuffed it in a stale bun along with some mustard. Rummaging around, I found a bag of potato chips and flat generic cola that Jeff had left out. Hardly a feast, but it would do. I had an old iPhone, years out of date, but it still worked well enough and got a signal. I watched a popular YouTuber talk about conspiracies as I ate and tried to relax.

Finishing, it was time for a shower. Under the water, cleaning off the day, I started thinking about the future. I hoped that future might have someone for me to love. An amalgam of women flashed in my head as my hand slid down between my legs. Summer, Lily, Liz, Keegan, even some pop stars and Hollywood actresses. None of it worked for me, I knew none of it was real. Swearing, I turned off the water and got out to find a relatively clean towel.

In one of Jeff's old tee shirts and a pair of clean underwear, I was back in bed and smoking a cigarette. One of these days I would quit. I knew I had to. I would do it for myself and Jade, not because I was told to. Jeff never understood that.

Ashing into a half empty water bottle, I peered around the room. It was a disaster, clustered and filthy. I idly wondered if I could ask Pith to destroy it along with all of Ennis. Utterly wiped off the map. As long the remaining members of my family were spared, I didn't care.

Three people, that's all that mattered to me. Three people and my unborn child.

I had to get through this.

Tessa would come back. I couldn't worry about her.

Liz would suffer. I couldn't savor her, but that was okay.

The Kin and the Throng would die. I could use them before they expired.

Everything would be fine.

I suppose part of me knew I was being overly optimistic, but I had to be. I had sacrificed so much; this was my way to a better life. If you have never been in poverty, never suffered cold and hunger, never been mocked for your lineage – things you can't always necessarily help – then you can't understand the pain and frustration. You would do just about anything to rise above, to change your station in life. Some manage to go to college, some turn to a life of crime. I was willing to take a few extra steps and participate in global genocide.

So, I personally killed a few dozen people, right? Who hasn't in the Carrion Court? Ah, but it was towards a greater end. That end was my salvation, so fuck you.

CHAPTER 49

DANIEL

Liz was still completely unconscious, but Keegan was starting to come around again. It had been about maybe half an hour; I wasn't really sure. Time was hard to calculate in our position.

I had made the most of it by trying to come up with a plan.

They didn't appear to have the numbers I had initially thought we'd be facing. That was a plus. On the minus side, they were wielding more powerful Sect magic than I had anticipated. That magic could be countered if we had the numbers back on our side. We either had to last long enough for reinforcements to find us or get those reinforcements here sooner. As for the latter, well, I had another terrible idea.

"Keegan? Keegan, wake up!"

She was already stirring, eyes fluttering, as she tilted her head to look at me. Something like a smile there, trying to mask the terror. I smiled back and leaned closer, the chains allowing for more leeway than I believe our captor realized. Our foreheads touched and for a moment, all the horrors faded away.

"You okay?" I asked.

A slight nod. "I think so."

"She fed on your fear."

"Yeah," whispered Keegan. "Made me feel hollow. And, I don't know, brittle? Like a husk. It's unpleasant but not painful, just overwhelming."

"She hasn't tried it on me, I'm too pissed off."

Keegan snorted a laugh. "What a shock."

"Listen, I have an idea, but you're going to hate it."

Keegan sighed. "Of course."

"I think our young friend was in too much of a hurry to get us chained up and didn't to it securely enough. We shouldn't be able to move this much, get this close. The only thing truly binding us in these shackles is the magic."

"Right, conveniently carved into are backs, if I'm not mistaken?"

"I think I can reach your back," I said.

She glanced up at my hands, cuffed above my head. "How you figure?"

"Not, uh... not with my hands. With my mouth."

Keegan leaned back. "What are you going to do with your mouth, Daniel?"

I couldn't look at her as I said it.

"Bite off a piece of the symbol."

She didn't say anything, just hung there. Without the psychic link, I was terrified she thought maybe I wanted one last chance to eat her before it was too late. Maybe she thought this was some double cross. I honestly had no idea. I had expected her to argue, to fight me on this, but not go silent. For some reason, it made me anxious. I was about to drop the whole idea and figure something else out.

"I'm sorry, we'll..."

"Do you honestly think it'll work?" she asked.

I shrugged. "It's the best thing I can think of."

Keegan looked me dead in in the eyes. "Please don't swallow me."

"I won't."

She twisted in her chains as best she could to face me and I stretched as far as my shackles would allow. It would be close. Straining, I could just get my teeth to a section of skin near her right shoulder blade. It was a portion cut with the symbol I was counting on being imbued with the magic. Tendons and muscles pushed to their limit, testing the limits of the chains, I began to gnaw away at Keegan's skin. She pulled away at first, but I said her name as gently as possible, and she returned to position. Another swipe of my teeth ground deeper into her flesh. I spat out what I was collecting in my mouth, determined to hold my promise to her. Her body shook with sobs as I took another bite out of her shoulder, feeling something pop in my neck as I forced myself to go deeper.

That last bite had an immediate effect.

Keegan's hair flared purple and I was thrown back against the wall with a psychic blast. All the chains and manacles holding her shattered, and she stepped away with glow engulfing her. Everything that had been bottled up inside her, that maelstrom of emotion, now surged around her.

"Keegan, look at me! Please!"

The colors and light began to subside, and the Throng manifestations left. She stood there breathing heavily and looking wildly around the room. I didn't have to read minds to know what she was thinking.

"There's no time, you have to go," I said to her.

"What? No, I can get you out!"

"You're not skilled enough in your powers. It might take you too long, or you might shatter my body in the process. No, just run! Go find a phone and get ahold of Rosenthal. Come back with the cavalry."

"Daniel..."

"Keegan, run!"

She snatched up a bloody but passable shirt that was sitting on one of the tables and quickly changed into it. She went to the door and peered out into the night. She would make it; I knew she would. As long as she was safe.

She took one look at back me. I smiled at her. "Go." Then she was gone.

I slumped in my chains, telling myself there was nothing more I could do now. I had to believe she would get away to contact Rosenthal and the others, and that they would return before I was dead. Even if that last part didn't happen, that was okay. I had run a good race, especially if my finish line was saving Keegan.

I knew that psycho little Sect girl was going to be mighty irate when she ventured in next. I'd likely be the recipient of some creative brutality. She'd be in for a surprise if she thought she'd get any fear out of me, especially now.

I'll be straight with you, it had been a tense few days, so at this point I fell asleep. It's not exactly heroic or badass, but I never claimed to be either or those.

INTERLUDE 5

The Ennis City Police Department was buzzing with activity, filled with various members of law enforcement, forensic techs stopping in, people from City Hall, the County, and even a phone call that morning from the Governor's Office. The Press were still lurking around ready to pounce on any lurid detail that would bring the tabloid ratings, and Dr. Wertz had given her professional opinion to a number of other individuals affiliated with the case.

Without any new leads, it was going to be in the hands of forensics. Unfortunately, science usually took longer that detective work, and there was a good chance that they'd have more bodies, dead or missing, before there were answers. No one involved was happy with that.

Kenyon saw Hayward sitting at a large desk the two had been given months ago to share at the beginning of the case. Most of their files were now in a conference room that the task force was meeting in, one he was technically part of, but one he and his partner had been largely shut out of. Chief McVay and Captain Long said they'd be kept "in the loop," but everyone knew what that was code for.

While Hayward had bristled at all the passive aggressive politics, Kenyon had played along. He smiled, shrugged, bought a few coffees, and shook a few hands. It had only taken a short time to gather information from people, and piece it together before the task force had.

Kenyon sat across from his partner grinning, holding a slim file folder.

"What are you so happy about?" asked Hayward.

"What to make a bust before the task force?"

Hayward leaned forward. "Very much so, yes."

"While you were being grumpy, I was working."

"Spill it."

"A long dark hair was found in the van."

"We already knew that."

"Yesterday, Elizabeth McCreary was reported as missing. It hasn't been a full 24 hours, but with things being the way they are around here, we're taking all reports seriously after twelve. She was last seen leaving work yesterday with a young woman with long dark hair."

"Now that's interesting."

"It gets better. That dark-haired girl was identified as Kelsey Radu."

Hayward rubbed his forehead. "Why do I know that name?"

"Her dad is Michael Radu, of Radu Towing. He owns his own private tow truck."

"Shit! That would explain where some of the vehicles are going, and even how victims are getting moved."

"Yep."

"Daughter and father in it together? Whole family, maybe?"

Kenyon held up his hands. "I've met Mike Radu a few times on calls. He seemed nice enough, but you know how it is. From what I hammered together, they're just another lower-class American family in Ennis trying to get by. Dad, mom, three daughters. Could be a grandma. They live up on the hill."

"Everybody on the hill is fucking weird, and you know it."

"True, but 'serial killing as a family hobby,' weird?"

"We need to check this out."

"Oh yeah."

Hayward got up first and went to the door, no one really paying him any attention. After Kenyon got another cup of coffee, he talked to the dispatcher for a moment, then made his way out. Fortunately, any of the people who would have asked too many questions or given them any grief were still in the task force meeting.

Outside, Hayward stood frowning beside his cruiser.

"What?" asked Kenyon.

"Should we take a personal vehicle?"

Kenyon thought about it for a second before shaking his head. "No. No, we want this to be legit."

"I'm not worried about it being legit, I'm more worrying about the element of surprise."

"I hadn't thought about that. I mean, if they're crazy enough to take a shot on cops, I'd rather have an extra radio in the car, along with the ones on us. Plus, the arsenal in the truck."

Hayward beamed. "I may get out the shotgun when we get there."

"I'm driving."

CHAPTER 50

KELSEY

I had only snagged a few hours of sleep, but it was better than nothing. No one had done laundry in weeks, so I slipped on a pair of yoga pants on inside out and pulled on one of Jeff's old zip up hoodies while I brewed a cup of coffee. I didn't bother with anything else on underneath, my mind wandering to Liz. Even the dark roast couldn't cover up the stench of the trailer. I'd come to consider it as the sharp aroma of despair.

Coffee in hand, it was time for the shack. I needed to reaffirm my position of authority with the Kin and the Throng, and toy with Liz for a few hours. Days would have been preferable, but I'd be lucky to have one.

I was taking a sip of my coffee when I rounded the corner, formulating some witty little quip to throw out to them. It all fell apart when I saw Keegan was gone, and Daniel smiling at me. Liz cowered there, head snapping back and forth between us silently.

"Good morning!" he said. "Did you bring coffee for us, too?"

I hurled the mug at his head and missed. "Where is she?"

His smile twisted, revealing something far more sinister, something I don't think I had fully expected.

"She's amassing an army, you stupid little bitch."

I stormed over and grabbed a knife off the table. Back at Liz, I held it to her throat. She sobbed and begged, until I smacked her on the head with the hilt.

"I will happily kill her unless you tell me where the Throng went."

Daniel laughed. "I don't care. I eat people for fun. If I got loose, I was going to eat her. Get my strength up and screw you over at the same time."

I sneered at him. I couldn't tell if I believed him or not. My own ignorance about Kin was definitely working against me. I knew they ate flesh, but how much, how often? He had seemed protective of Keegan, but was that simply because she was a Throng?

"Let me clear this up for you," he said. "You're what, seventeen or eighteen? I'm a lot older than what I look. Kin don't age the same way Sect do. I don't give a damn how many you've killed in your adorable little spree. I've still murdered and eaten at least three times as many. By all means, slice up the ginger. I'll still be waiting on my coffee and the coming reinforcements."

Something snapped. Maybe it was his confidence or the way he talked down to me. It doesn't matter. Gripping that knife, I began to do exactly as he stated.

Liz's screams echoed through the shack.

The blade tore into her, stabbing and slicing. My rage and frustration behind every thrust, blood splattering everywhere. Liz, my mom, Jeff, the world, everything that had disappointed and failed me. At some point I realized I was screaming as well, tears streaming down my face. It shook me out of my frenzy long enough to realize that Liz was almost dead. Almost completely wasted.

I grabbed her face and sucked out her fear. Not very much, not nearly enough. In the back of the shack, I deposited it in Ruby, shaking and pissed. Yes, pissed at the Kin, but more pissed at myself. He had worked me up, hitting all the right nerves.

Sure enough, Liz was dead. All those years, all those fantasies gone. I didn't know how to feel.

I heard a car door slam and started out towards the front of the shack. Fortunately, I hesitated, and glanced out before exiting. It was a police car. Two officers looking around. Of all the god damn times. The taller one gestured my way, and the bald one started ambling down towards the shack.

Running over I grabbed a wad of Liz's bloody clothing off the ground and stuffed it into Daniel's mouth before he knew what was happening. Without slowing down, I hit the lights, and dove into the back of the room, hoping the gloom and Ruby would keep me hidden.

Maybe he didn't notice the lights go out. Maybe he was at the wrong angle. Chances were that he was too concerned about what he saw when he walked into the room.

"Jesus Christ," he said, his gun drooping from a firing stance.

I could see his eyes go from Liz to Daniel then back to Liz. As I assumed, he found Liz to be the more immediate concern. She was a young woman, and Daniel had no apparent injuries. Kneeling down, he holstered his weapon.

"Miss, are you okay?" he asked, checking for vital signs.

That's when I sprung.

I only needed to make it a few paces.

The cop heard me move and looked up.

A few more feet and I was there.

He started reaching for his gun.

My hand raised, words on my lips.

His gun left his holster.

Two more steps.

He aimed.

"Dashoon."

The barrel-chested bald cop fell to the ground asleep. I didn't bother wasting any time. I pulled him off out of the way and slit his throat against the wall. I wasn't taking any chances. Not this late in the game. His gun had fallen off to the side, and it went up on the table with all my other tools.

I was about to make a snarky remark to Daniel when a gunshot went off. Before I could react, the Kin managed to spat out his makeshift gag and licking a bit of the blood residue off his lips. He looked more amused than before.

"Gee, you're having a real crap day, aren't you?"

CHAPTER 51

DANIEL

The cops were unexpected. I didn't know if they were Keegan's doing or not at the time. Honestly, Kelsey didn't seem all that stable, so I wouldn't have been surprised if the authorities had tracked her down eventually. She was sloppy in a fashion that Kin Elders would've never abided. I wondered if the Sect Elders knew about her schemes.

A short but robust middle-aged man came in lugging another cop. I had to hand it to the guy, he was beast. He was bleeding from a gunshot wound to the shoulder, yet still managed to subdue and haul the cop down here. The cop was bleeding from a nasty gash on the head, completely out cold.

"Dad, are you okay?" exclaimed Kelsey.

"I'll be fine," said the guy. "We need to deal with this."

So, the whole family was involved. Were they all Sect? I was going to have to be damn careful. I watched as the cop was chained up beside me where Keegan had once been, never regaining consciousness.

"Well, I suppose he'll make up for the Throng," said Kelsey.

Her dad frowned. "What happened to her?"

"I don't know."

A grimace of pain. "Maybe the bones?"

"That's an idea. I'll talk to grandma."

"I'll tell you what happened," I said. "She got loose, and she's bringing a ton of angry, hungry Kin back here."

Daddy punched me in the face. That got me laughing, and I asked for seconds. He went to do it again, but Kelsey stopped him. She knew she wasn't getting any fear out of me, but I couldn't figure out why she hadn't simply killed me yet.

"Leave the other bodies where they are. They might jumpstart Officer... Hayward when he wakes up. We're running out of time," said Kelsey as she left with her dad.

I gave it about fifteen minutes. I figured by that point they were back up the house, Kelsey applying first aid on her dad. Time to wake up Hayward.

I rocked back in forth in my chains, attempting to jostle him. Saying his name as loud as I dared, I tried kneeing him, too. I couldn't hit him very hard; he had been done up tighter than Keegan had been. After about ten minutes, he started to come around.

"Wha... where am I?'

"You're being held prisoner in a murder shed."

"What?"

"You got captured by hillbilly witches."

"Kenyon?"

"Who's that? Oh, your partner? Sorry, man."

"What?"

I tilted my head over towards the wall. I could tell it was taking Hayward a moment for his eyes to focus. Then another moment for his brain to process. Then the rage came.

"Mother fuckers!"

"Yeah, I know. But you've got to calm down for a second, okay? Let me explain to you what we're up against."

"Who the fuck are you?"

I sighed. "My name's Daniel, and I'm captured exactly like you."

His face softened a bit. "Sorry, right."

"Officer Hayward, this whole thing is being orchestrated by Kelsey Radu, the daughter. There's at least three others – dad, mom, and a grandma."

"Should be and older and younger sister, too."

"I haven't seen a younger sister, but, eh, I think that might be the older sister back there."

Hayward turned his head to make out what he could of the corpse lovingly preserved and hanging in the back. I could hear him mutter something and look down at the ground. His eye found Liz not far away.

"Who was she?"

"I know her name was Liz, that's it."

"Jesus."

"Listen, we just have to hold out for a while. I assume if you're here, that means the authorities are closing in. Plus, there are other, let's say 'factions,' that are on their way."

"Kenyon and I were working on our own tip. It could take them days. Sure, each cruiser is lowjacked, but all they have to do is move it. They seem good at that, given the state of that garage. I mean, there are other..."

"I have people, don't worry."

Hayward side-eyed me. "Like who?"

"You could say I'm an independent contractor, hired to find the Radus. Their killing spree hadn't gone unnoticed by my employers. Of course, getting caught wasn't part of the plan. But I had an associate, and she got free last night. Right now, she's getting backup."

I'd like to say that I was personally proud of that spin I'd put on things.

"So what, some kind of private security firm?"

"I suppose they would see themselves like that, sure."

"Facing off against a family of serial killers in Ohio? Isn't that a little below your pay grade?"

"Don't for one second underestimate the Radu family," I said. "They are sadistic and violent, and more powerful that you would believe. The family is operating under delusional religious beliefs, fueling their need to kill. We're talking an apocalyptic cult here, who will do anything to achieve their goals, Officer Hayward. Your partner's already seen it in full."

Hayward gritted his teeth and nodded. I hadn't outright lied to the man, but I'd told him what he'd needed to stay alive and believe the real threat we were up against. I didn't know what we'd see first – the human authorities, the Kin, or death. Regardless, it seemed out of our hands now.

At this point, I recall hoping Kelsey's day continued to be crap.

CHAPTER 52

KELSEY

Things were officially beginning to spiral out of control.

I helped my dad back to the house and got him into a chair in the kitchen. Because it was the Radu house, the first aid supplies weren't in any one central location for convenience. It took another ten minutes of tearing through the house and gathering things up before I could start working on him.

Even after I got his flannel shirt off, I only had a faint idea of what I was supposed to be doing. Get the bullet out if hadn't gone all the way through, right? I checked for that, but I didn't see an exit would. That meant I had to dig for it. I went to town went the tweezers, my dad holding back a scream. Blood poured out of him, and he started to go white.

"Dad, stop! Hold on, I'm trying!"

"You're thinking like a human, girl," said my grandma, rolling her wheelchair in.

Coming up next to us, she yanked to tweezers out of my hand and set them on the table. Interlocking my fingers with hers, she placed my hand over my dad's wound and began chanting. Instinctively the words flowed through me and I knew them, chanted them with her. He roared in pain, but I felt something shoot up into my palm. The spent bullet. I tossed it to the ground and attended to the injury while my grandma retrieved a bottle a whiskey for my dad.

"I'm sorry I wasn't faster," he said.

"I'm sorry I brought this upon you," I replied.

"Not your fault."

"Isn't it?"

"Don't talk like that," said my grandma, handing the bottle to my dad. "This is a glorious mission, and you knew it was going to be a hard road. Of course, it was going to be rougher near the end, obstacles becoming more treacherous. That's the way of things."

"Are you going to have enough fear?" my dad asked.

I didn't say anything because I didn't know.

"You have quite a number in the shack and that should..." began my grandma.

"I have two. The Throng escaped somehow and most are dead."

"Damnation. That doesn't bode well."

"No, and the Kin is fearless, fueled by rage and an appreciation for violence. I have one cop, the other dead. The girl I brought is dead, although I did feed off her a couple times. I fed off of the Throng, too, but not enough. I don't know.

"Another hunt?" offered my dad.

I wrapped the bandages a little tighter and he winced. The blood was staining them but didn't appear to be leaking through. The salve I had applied really did work wonders. I worried about him chasing the stolen Vicodin my grandma had rustled up with another swig of whiskey, but I didn't say anything.

"I don't know if we have time for another hunt. Plus, we don't know what's going on out there. Are the Kin really coming? Do the authorities know our names? If I had some clue of how close I was, I could make better decisions here."

That was the major hurdle I was facing. I knew I was close, but just not how close. Magic is an art, not a science, and things are done by feel. Was I at ninety-five percent or ninety-nine percent? If I was only at ninety-five, I would need three people by my estimations. If I were closer, at say ninety-nine, the cop I already had captured would fill the vessel up to capacity. This near to completion, it was as if I wouldn't know until I was done.

Would there be some celestial event when it did happen? Would Pith manifest in Ruby, glowing and all-powerful, smiting all these enemies who inched in closer from every side? I had to believe that, to see a future not only beyond Ennis but beyond the next few days.

"Has Tessa come back yet?" I asked.

My grandma fiddled with a teacup. "No. As much as we tried to prepare her, I don't think she was quite ready for what it meant to be Sect. She always did cling a bit strongly to her human life."

"Where do you think she is?" asked my dad.

"Likely down in town, with her friends. Pretending to be one of them."

I sighed. "Maybe it's for the best. She'd be of no use during all this. I want to assume she's safe, wherever she is. We're going to have an outcome here shortly."

"Kelsey..." My dad began. "Hopefully we're alive to find her after that."

My nerves were on edge. I pushed a chair over to the sink and climbed up to a cupboard above it, one I knew my mom couldn't reach and wouldn't bother scaling up to. I had stashed a pack of cigarettes up there almost two years ago. Undoubtedly stale and would taste terrible, but at that second, I just needed my fix.

Lighting up off the stove, my dad rolled his eyes at me, but I ignored him. I needed to come up with some way to obtain a few more people, quick and easily. It would be great if I could order some pizzas to be delivered, but none of the local places would risk their drivers coming this far up the hill. Most of the roads were too bad. I thought about who else I could call and scam into coming up here. I didn't want any emergency services, I wanted civilians. Maybe plumbers or electricians?

Even then, with it all crumbling around me, I didn't feel like I had made a mistake.

Even now, standing here, I don't feel like I made a mistake then.

CHAPTER 53

DANIEL

Hayward had more questions. I should have expected as much, given that he was a detective. Things were getting dicey however because he starting to get increasingly curious about the Radu family and what they were up to. I was doing my best to dance around some of the more delicate subjects, but he knew I was evading him.

"What aren't you telling me?"

"I've been telling you stuff for the last hour, man."

"You're also, keeping something from me. I'm guessing a lot of things. Considering we're both about to get gutted by these hilljacks, care to share? So I actually know what I'm up against?"

Kelsey could return at any time, and he was going to see firsthand. so, I figured I might as well spill. He wasn't going to believe me anyway. Plus, it was going to provide some minor entertainment.

"Remember how I said they had delusional religious beliefs, and later you said you brought in a professor who verified she'd never seen practices like it before or something? Well, they're not so delusional. They're Witches, like actual Witches, pre-dating Christianity, not human Witches. Actually, a race called the Sect."

Hayward blinked at me. "Are you fucking kidding me?"

"The Sect look like humans, are human in most way, except they can harness magic and fed on fear. They've been around since the dawn of humanity, right under your nose. it's easy enough for them to hide. They torture humans and suck the fear out of them. Think Vampires with blood, that's usually the analogy used."

"You're insane."

"Would you feel better if I told you there are different kinds of monsters out there?" I said with a grin. "I'm one of the other groups. The other groups are pissed."

"If you didn't want to tell me, you could have come up with a more convincing…"

"Shhh!"

There was a rustle outside and a slight bang against the building. Usually Kelsey strolled right in, and my kind would have been far stealthier. Someone was attempting to sneak around and doing a bad job.

A head popped around the corner and I didn't know how to react.

"Keegan, what are you doing here!"

Keegan rushed into the room, her arms raised in what I'm guessing she thought was an offensive position. "Saving your ass."

"Who's this?" asked Hayward.

We looked at each other.

"Partner?" I replied.

"Works for me," she said, going for a knife. "Spin your back to me."

"What the hell?" exclaimed Hayward.

"We have spells on us," I tried, as she pulled the blade through by skin.

Nothing. It instantly healed back up.

"Did you call anybody? Rosenthal?"

Keegan nodded. "I got down the hill and flagged down a car. I got ahold of him through his business listing on the internet. He said there'd be a god damn army here by early afternoon, but… I couldn't wait. I couldn't leave you."

For the first time in decades, I felt a swell of emotion so strong that it welled up in my eyes. I felt it in my core. I wanted to hold her so badly. Protect her, cherish her, and I knew it wasn't because of her power. It was because of who she was.

"Get me down from here," I whispered.

She pulled at the shackles some more, frustrated. "I'm not eating part of your back."

I winked at Hayward. "Use your power."

"Uh, you sure?" she said, glancing at the officer.

"Yeah."

"C'mon guys, this is…"

Keegan lit up purple and pink. A burst of energy radiated off her fingertips and onto my back, searing the skin there, eradicating the symbol. It hurt, but not enough to stop me from glancing over my shoulder and catching the look on Hayward's face.

Priceless.

The chains shattered as I pulled them from the wall, partially transforming. Tapped into The Mist once more, I felt at full strength as I had been. Whatever the Sect had done, it had simply cut me off, not actually weakened me. Changing back, I immediately embraced Keegan.

"I'm okay," she said into my ear.

"I know."

"What the fuck is going on?" bellowed Hayward.

"Detective Hayward," I said, "This is Keegan Pembroke. She's a Throng, also, known as a Faerie. I'm a Kin, sometimes called a Wendigo. We're part of a supernatural organization called the Carrion Court here to stop a rogue, homicidal family of Sect. Do you want to kill some Witches?"

He stared at them, a mix of terror, awe, and confusion.

"He's asking if you're cool," said Keegan.

Hayward snorted and then began laughing. "Yeah, I'm cool. I don't know how much help I'm going to be up against Witches, especially alongside you two, but I'm game. If anything, I'll do it for Kenyon. He deserved better."

I reached up, tore down the chains and pulled apart the manacles holding him in place. It was obvious he was terrified of me, but he did his best to keep it under wraps. In an attempt to give him some equilibrium, I retrieved both side arms off the table and handed them to him.

"I had a shotgun in the cruiser, too,"

"No time. We're taking the house now," I said.

"What's the plan?"

"We hit it fast before they have a chance to retaliate. Kill everyone you see. Are you comfortable with that? Both of you?"

"Works for me," said Hayward.

Keegan stared at the ground.

"Keegan?"

"Unfortunately, yes," replied Keegan. "These people have to be stopped. I hate it, I hate what we're doing, but... this is true evil. There's no redemption here, no saving them."

"Keegan, I'm sorry you have to be a part of this. You can wait until Rosenthal arrives. Hell, we all can."

"No, they might run if you're found missing. More might die, and then that would be my fault."

"Let's go," say Hayward, moving toward the door.

Nearing the door, it hit me how much Keegan had risked coming back for me. How much this place scared her. How much she was compromising her principles because she knew, ultimately, what we were about to do was for the greater good. It all made me ache for her.

It made me love her.

The sunlight streaming down, catching the purple in her hair, she looked back at me with a smile. "I heard that."

CHAPTER 54

KELSEY

The stupid bandages were slipping, so I put my cigarette out in the sink and walked back over to my dad to adjust them. I could tell he wasn't faring well, even with the booze and pills. I didn't personally know any healing magic, but knew my grandma dabbled in that spectrum.

I was about to ask her about it when the door splintered in with a crash.

It's my own fault really. Too many distractions, too many concerns. I had been juggling an impossible number of factors from the beginning. I was so stupid.

The Kin came tearing into the house in full Wendigo form before any of us could react. I have no problem admitting he was absolutely terrifying. Something about that pale skin, gaping jaw, and those unnatural antlers. He turned to take in all of us, but it was my grandma who found the strength to start chanting.

For a moment, I felt victory rush through me, but it didn't last long. The cop and the Throng raced in. The cop raised his guns and got off two shots, but I used my magic to hurl the weapons from his hands. With a growl, he tackled my dad, and they began to grapple on the kitchen floor. I looked up at the Throng in time to see her use her powers to throw me across the room.

I was done getting thrown across rooms.

My dad was trading punch for punch with the cop, and my grandma appeared to barely have the Kin held in place. Pulling myself up, I touched my belly and scowled. This Faerie bitch was going to learn.

I reached up and brought part of the ceiling down, trying to crush her, but she leapt out of the way. She tried getting in my head, I think, but I shook it off and went for a different tactic. I tried to get closer to her to use the sleeping spell on her, but it was like she knew what I was up to and backed around closer to the door.

"You're right," she said. "I am in your head. I know what you're going to do before you do it."

Her skin turning pink, she flung out her arm and the table shattered, startling everyone.

It was all the Kin needed. He took two steps forward, ripping his claws up through my grandma, through her stomach and chest, her head flying off is a gush off blood. The wheelchair bashed against the wall, leaving streaks of red on the floor.

I heard myself screaming.

I was beyond caring at that point.

Channeling what powers of Pith I could, I imposed my god's will upon the beast. Forced the Voice, the dominion, the madness. If this Kin wanted to ravage and kill, then it would. It would be feral forever.

The Kin roared and stomped around, smashing everything in sight. The Throng backed up, instantly realizing something had changed. The cop didn't possess the same clarity. He staggered too close into the monster's radius and was snatched up. Before he could react in any meaningful way, his throat was bitten out. Lifted high, his whole abdomen was devoured there in the entrance to the living room.

"You did this to him!" screamed the Throng, tears streaming down.

"Imagine what I'm going to do to you."

My dad had started to get up, broken and bruised, but still alive. At least I still had him. I would finish this here with the Throng, then finish the mission. Perhaps I'd allow the Kin the live – let it rampage through Ennis for a few hours.

It was something on that Faerie bitch's face. I should've seen it.

"I can't let you win," she said.

"What are you going to do?"

With a flourish of her hand, she lifted my dad off the ground and brought him down hard onto the broken remnants of the table, impaling him in two places.

I screamed. I ran. I held my dad as he died.

The Kin was still eating the cop, occasionally snarling at us. The Throng simply stared at me in silence.

Tears poured down my face. "I'm going to kill you."

"I know."

I lunged at her, my hands around her neck. I summoned every iota of magic I had and began to suck the fear from her. The life from her. Everything that made Keegan Pembroke who she was, I drained. I clawed it out of her, down in every corner. I took her soul.

Her body turned gray, her hair brittle. I dropped her, the body now only a husk. I had to get to Ruby, get this power inside the vessel. I hadn't made it a single step when I heard the wailing behind me. The Kin. He was transforming back, making his way over to the body. Somehow her death must have broken my spell.

I didn't have time to worry about that. I had a massive amount of fear inside me, a good chance enough to complete the ritual. Sprinting out the door, I left the pathetic animal sobbing over the corpse of his girl.

CHAPTER 55

DANIEL

Keegan.

I wanted to believe that this was some other form Throng could take, some defensive mechanism or something. That maybe she was just in a coma or astral projecting, or who the hell knew what. I needed her to wake up in my arms. No more of this gray, blotchy skin, and dry hair falling out. Her bloodshot eyes could stop looking in the wrong directions. She could stop being so limp, so boneless.

She was going to be fine.

Except she wasn't.

And I knew that.

I gently laid her back down. Sitting there naked and covered in blood, I knew Kelsey had bolted out of the house only a minute or two ago. Part of me didn't care. I didn't care about my assignment anymore, that was for sure. I did care about revenge, however. She might try to escape, but even if she tried to flee, she'd likely go one place first.

Through the yard and up to the outbuilding where I had been held captive. We had been held. Rage ran through me. I didn't care what happened to me at this point, as long as Kelsey Radu died as well.

Stepping inside, I could hear her in the back, pleading with the corpse strung up. She was stroking its face, like it was a lover.

"Please, that should've been enough! That's all there is, and time's running out."

"Time's up."

She spun around and sneered at me.

"I'm going to rip that baby out of you with my bare hands and make you watch as I eat it."

She spit on the floor. "Wendigo filth. You all should've been exterminated."

"And the Throng, too?" I screamed. "Did she need to die?"

Kelsey's eyes narrowed. "She killed my dad."

"And all those humans? And the…"

"Everyone! I'll kill everyone, do you understand?"

"Yeah, I think I do, you psychotic piece of white trash Sect."

She began chanting as I shot across the room. Neither of us achieved much before whispers filled the space, dropping both of us to our knees. The agony was unbearable, and I think I went into a petite mal seizure. Through it, I could vaguely make out Kelsey. There was a trickle of blood running out of her nose.

The whispers lessened, and gradually I found myself standing up. I wasn't the one controlling myself, though. From the look on her face, Kelsey was experiencing the same effect. We both march stiffly outside.

There were easily over a hundred individuals in attendance. A gathering that hadn't been there moments ago.

Close to the building we had emerged from were about two dozen with glowing red eyes. Vampires. I'm guessing they had used their influence to control us. I was aware that the Sallow weren't vulnerable to sunlight like the legends would have humans believe, but I had never really thought about it much. The whispers came from their lips.

Out among the crowd, I could pick out a couple dozen with purple hair, my heart broke seeing them. Keegan would never know her people. Moving towards the front, there off to the left, were Rosenthal and Mayumi. With them were a few other Kin I recognized.

My sorrow turned once more to rage. "Where the fuck were all of you?"

A tall, slender man separated from the crowd, his eyes flashing red. He was dressed in a three-piece charcoal suit with a crimson tie, his blonde hair brushed back. Angular and handsome, he took in the surrounding as if it was all a normal day.

"Mr. Hale, it's a pleasure to meet you. I am Gaspard Laurent, Chancellor of the Carrion Court. We've been monitoring this entire event as it has unfolded."

"Monitoring? If you had been here fifteen minutes early, Keegan Pembroke would still be alive!"

"We mourn with the Throng for their fallen sister, but it could not be avoided. Certain precautions had to be taken, certain possibilities avoided."

"Rosenthal, what is he babbling about?"

I saw Rosenthal start to come down the hill, but Laurent held out a hand, and Mayumi stopped him. I had no idea what was going on. Examining the collective, I could easily make out Sallow and Throng, no doubt more of my own Kin among them, too. Were there Sect up there as well? What of the Djinn?

Kelsey laughed. "Now what? You can't stop me. Even now, it's too late. I know it is! You're all going to be cleansed off this new world, my new world! You'll see."

"Do shut up, child," said Laurent.

The cavalry had come, just too late to matter. Keegan was dead, the mission in flames. Kelsey seemed to think she had won, but I didn't know what that meant. At that moment, I didn't care. If I had been able to move, I would've killed Kelsey Radu and let the Court do whatever they wanted to me. I'm pretty sure they knew that.

Laurent sighed. "We will not allow a civil war to break out among the Tribes and disrupt the Carrion Court. Specifically, I speak of a conflict between the Kin and the Sect. To appease both sides, the two of you are being indefinitely detained."

"You have no right!" shrieked Kelsey.

"We have every right."

"I was given Longtooth status by Elder Mayumi," I said.

"Yes, to kill other Kin, not to kill Sect."

"The Sect were attacking all of us!"

"Then you should have verified your findings and reported it back to the Elders."

"But..." I began, then stopped.

"Acts of aggression by both offending parties have been reviewed in a critical manner, Mr. Hale."

I chuckled. "You know full well what happened, but I'm just a political scapegoat; Hell, so is she. Instead of taking the appropriate actions, you're going to say we were all acting rogue so you can cover it up and keep everything tidy. The Elders keep their peace and power."

"I'm sure I don't know what you're talking about," replied Laurent.

"You can't get me out of here without a fight," said Kelsey.

"Perhaps I can't," said Laurent. "But the Vacant can."

Kelsey's eyes went wide as a shimmer appeared before us, something like millions of fragments of broken glass caught in a storm. That gleam caught the light, silver and gold, and a broad shouldered, dark-skinned man stood there. His body had a metallic sheen to it, his eyes all black. Something about his proportion were off, his face almost alien in design. The Djinn lived up to everything I had heard.

Without emotion, he reached out and I felt the world fall away.

Keegan.

*   *   *

And you know everything after that.

I ended up in a cell beneath the Carrion Court citadel, routinely dragged out in front of this lovely group of Elders to tell my story from the beginning. I don't know why you've bothered. It's already been made abundantly clear to me that I'm a political prisoner, held to keep the Sect happy. Did you ever bother to punish the Sect, or even investigate? No, of course not.

I just have one question. If Kelsey Radu is still alive, tell me she's still imprisoned, too.

Good.

EPILOGUE

My esteemed Elders of the Carrion Court, we have now heard the testimony of both our brother Kin, Daniel Hale, and our sister Sect, Kelsey Radu. Their words have been verified by a psychic link provided by Elder Throng, Erin O'Malley. It has been recorded in both digital and mystical fashion, now sealed in accordance with security protocols.

We are here to go over some final matters and close this affair.

The Sect have agreed for sanctions against Elders Annette, Masozi, and Eloa for their part in the plot. The terms of which shall be determined with the Court's approval. These repercussions have enabled a mollification from the Kin and the Throng. It may take time for there to be trust again between us, but we will have peace now.

The budding Sect, Tessa Radu, was never found despite our efforts. We believe her innocent of any wrong-doing in these incidents, but still are uneasy with her disappearance. It is unclear whether she is dead by some unknown means or if she's simply fled. Periodic attempts will be made to locate her.

Daniel Hale and Kelsey Radu remain in our custody. It is currently our position that they will live out the rest of their natural lives imprisoned here. While some feel it would be more justified to execute them, opposing factions would see them freed as heroes. Martyrs are not needed on either side, so they will live, hopefully to be forgotten one day.

Kelsey Radu will give birth to her child in captivity. It will not be named Jade Radu, but instead given to another Sect family to be raised as their own. The daughter will never know her mother. Kelsey Radu does not know this.

Finally, and most disturbing.

A mystical talisman in the form of a corpse that we now know was a vessel that Kelsey Radu believed she could use as a conduit to manifest the Sect god Pith into disappeared en route on its way to the citadel. Details are scant, as everyone involved with the transport is in a vegetative state – Throng and Vampire both. We do have some human eyewitness accounts, stating that a naked young woman with symbols drawn all over her body climbed out of the back of the truck and ran into the woods.

Interesting to note, she had purple hair.

END

ABOUT THE AUTHOR

Brian Fatah Steele has been writing various types of dark fiction for over fifteen years, from horror to urban fantasy and science fiction. Steele originally went to school for fine arts but finds himself far more fulfilled now by storytelling. His short stories appear in anthologies such as 4POCALYPSE, BLOOD TYPE, DEATH'S REALM, THE IDOLATERS OF CTHULHU, PAYING THE FERRYMAN, CTHULHU LIES DREAMING, and the Bram Stoker Award-nominated DARK VISIONS, VOL.1. His sci-fi/horror novel THERE IS DARKNESS IN EVERY ROOM was published by Sinister Grin Press in March of 2017, and his cosmic horror/urban fantasy novel BLEED AWAY THE SKY was published by Bloodshot Books in January of 2019. His cosmic horror/urban fantasy novel, CELESTIAL SEEPAGE, was published by Alien Agenda Press in October of 2019, while his creature-feature novella HUNGRY RAIN was published by Severed Press in May of 2020. His self-published titles include YOUR ARMS AROUND ENTROPY, BRUTAL STARLIGHT, FURTHER THAN FATE, and IN BLEED COUNTRY.

https://www.amazon.com/Brian-Fatah-Steele/e/B002V7OJR0/

https://twitter.com/brian_f_steele

https://www.facebook.com/brianfatahsteele

ALSO FROM BLOODSHOT BOOKS

EVERY BLOODLINE HAS SECRETS

Audrey Darrow lost her mother when she was a child. Now, her absent father has passed away and now Elliot, the half-brother she never knew, wants to connect with the only family he has left on an impromptu cross-country road trip.

BUT SOME SECRETS ARE BEST LEFT HIDDEN

Soon after the journey begins, she learns that her mother belonged to an ancient line of women - women who held powers they used to seal and protect our realm from an onslaught of nightmarish entities - and Audrey is the last of them.

AND YOU CAN'T FLEE THE PAST FOREVER

Now a mystic cabal is determined to force her into her role, while a parade of otherworldly creatures attempt to kill her in order to end her line forever. Audrey must decide how to deal with the strange blood in her lineage, and about whether the world is worth saving or not... before it's too late

Available in paperback or Kindle on Amazon.com

http://bit.ly/BleedPB

Missing for seven months , fifteen-year-old Ted Wallace wakes by the river with no memory of where he has been or what has transpired during his absence. He only wants his life to return to normal, but soon he realizes the chaos that his disappearance caused, and that his return has only made matters worse.

His sister, feeling like an outcast from the family, finds solace in old friends and becomes a victim of horrendous bullying at school.

His mother is torn apart by conflicting emotions: concern for Ted given his life-long heart condition and anger about his disappearance which she diverts towards the local oddball.

Worst of all, his father, no longer able to contain his drinking problem, becomes convinced that the boy who has been returned is not his son at all, but a doppelganger with an insidious purpose.

As other missing persons return, Ted discovers where he has been and what he must do, but the sinister influences around his family threaten to tear them all to pieces before he can do what is necessary to bring their lives back to normal.

Available in paperback or Kindle on Amazon.com

https://amzn.to/31zuePs

HALLOWEEN, 1988

A gang of twelve-year-old boys are trick-or-treating in London. Off in the distance, they hear the discordant chimes of an ice-cream truck. It seems strange to hear on a cold autumnal night, but their thoughts of maximizing their candy haul soon dismissed its incongruous melody... until they saw the rusting hulk idling in the shadows at the end of the street, its driver a faceless shadow.

That was the night he took one of them.

OCTOBER, 2016

Years later, Halloween is fast approaching and Tom Craven is still haunted by the events of that dark night, especially the fact that their friend was never found. Increasingly plagued by horrific visions, Tom returns to the place where it all began, only to discover he's not the only one who can feel it. His friends have already arrived and are preparing for a battle which could get them all killed.

The Ice Cream Man is back... *and he's come for the ones that got away.*

Available in paperback or Kindle on Amazon.com

https://amzn.to/2YihXkt

CIVILIZATION HAS FALLEN...

The GAG Virus has infected most of humanity, stripping the consciousness from the host body and transforming innocent people into belligerent Ghosts and rabid Ghouls.

BUT ONE GIRL DOESN'T KNOW...

Near the remains of Cleveland, Ohio, Abbey's father has managed her agoraphobia and kept her safe from the apocalypse for four years by maintaining a fragile refuge of fantasy and denial...an elaborate blanket fort spanning the upper floors of an apartment building.

UNTIL HER FATHER DIES...

Now, his unhinged spirit reveals to Abbey that the world Outside is a wasteland populated by rampaging creatures, demented phantoms, and merciless scavengers. On her own for the first time in her life, she must find the courage to defend her beloved Fort from her father's undead corpse, from the ruthless stranger who murdered him, and from creatures more terrifying than anything she has ever imagined...and in turn find her true destiny.

Available in paperback or Kindle on Amazon.com

ON THE HORIZON FROM
BLOODSHOT BOOKS
2020-21*

Soundtrack to the End of the World – Anthony J. Rapino

Marmalade – Roland Blackburn

BioTerror – Tim Curran

Birthright – Christine Morgan

Cracker Jack – Asher Ellis

The Obese – Jarred Martin

Cluster – Renee Miller

Pound of Flesh – D. Alexander Ward

Crimson Springs – John Quick

Popsicle – Christa Wojciechowski

Schafer – Timothy G. Huguenin

Revival Road – Chris DiLeo

The Amazing Alligator Girl – Kristin Dearborn

Fairlight – Adrian Chamberlin

Ungeheuer – Scott A. Johnson

Teach Them How to Bleed – L.L. Soares

Blood Mother: A Novel of Terror – Pete Kahle

BLOODSHOT
BOOKS

READ UNTIL YOU BLEED!